EMERGENCE

SEVER THE CROWN BOOK 1

LINDSEY R. LOUCKS, MYSTI
PARKER

DEDICATION

To Anne Rice and Charlaine Harris, who inspired my love of vampires. And to all the authors who are paving the way for a myriad of voices in romance. ~Mysti

To all the vampires I've met. P.S. My neck is still available. ~ Lindsey

CHAPTER ONE

WREN

ANOTHER TOWN, ANOTHER GIG in a smoky dive, another name to cross off my list. At least two such names were regulars at The Sundowner Bar. One happened to be sitting at a booth. He was already drunk before I opened the show. That would make things easier when the time came.

I sang, but the lyrics were on autopilot. Good thing, too, considering how my mind swirled with memories, repeating its own chorus: *They killed your mother. Show no mercy.*

It helped to repeat the facts to myself so emotion didn't jack up my plans: Rusty Grimes, Rt. 2 Box 295, Silversage, Alabama. Age forty-two, weight approximately 310 lbs. Carries a 44 Magnum with Remington hollow-point silver-tipped bullets.

Torn vinyl seats made a squeaky fart noise every time Rusty shifted or got up to take a piss. This redneck smelled like sour pickles and gun grease. But they all shared the same subtle scent of rotten fish and old blood

– they certainly had enough blood on their hands, figuratively speaking.

Rusty's phone buzzed, the ring tone some power-to-the-rednecks Toby Keith bullshit. He picked it up, put it to his ear. I homed in on the conversation between songs:

"Yeah, what?"

A woman answered. "Where you at?" She had a phlegmy voice that sounded like a three-packs-a-day kinda gal.

Sometimes having a super sense of hearing was more curse than gift.

"Just stopped for a drink. What d'ya need?"

"You drunk?"

"Naw."

Liar *and* murderer. Quite the resume.

"Can you get some Taco Bell? I want one o' them big chicken burritas."

"Yeah, okay, what for the kids?"

So he had reproduced. I couldn't imagine who would want to see him naked. She must have been hideous.

"McDonald's nuggets, large fry, apple pies."

"All right. Ya got dranks?"

"Yeah, got some Meller Yellers."

"Okay." He put down the phone, chugged down the rest of his Coors, then belched and wiped his mouth with his sleeve.

Well. The man had a family. They didn't know he wouldn't be coming home tonight. A twinge of guilt plucked at my eye and made it twitch. In another second, the moment passed. My mother had a child too. And she'd been the only family I ever had.

They killed your mother. Show no mercy.

No matter how badly I wanted to fly off that stage and rip his head off, I had to be patient. There could be no witnesses. I just wished my damn wig wasn't so scratchy and hot. It had looked much better on the mannequin head - a black chin-length bob that went well with my southern grunge act. The brown suede high-heeled boots weren't my favorite, but they worked with the half denim, half calico patchwork skirt. The shirt was a favorite, a long-sleeved tight black hooded pullover with thumb cuffs. Black eye shadow, falsies, brown contact lenses, and dark red lipstick completed the illusion.

My band consisted of me, my Fender Stratocaster electric guitar, and whatever backup musicians I could afford to hire locally. In the tiny write-ups in newspaper entertainment sections, they said things like, "Melody Songsmith's voice is an eclectic mix between Janis Joplin and Bonnie Raitt – gritty, bluesy, and unapologetic." I'm not sure about that, but I often performed their songs and got totally lost in them.

Tonight's crowd-pleaser was the Joplin hit, "Me and Bobby McGee". I rocked out to the high-energy chorus, fingers tapping to the beat on the mic. My body shimmied, shook, and swung uncontrollably to the music like a woman possessed by a rock-n-roll demon. My voice resonated through the speakers, mouth open wide, eyes squeezed shut. We brought it home – the kind of finale that conjured up goose pimples on anyone who paid attention.

Applause rang out as the final notes faded. Rusty lifted his Coors bottle high in the air and hooted his appreciation. I grinned at him, perhaps a little too long. He went quiet, his smile sinking into a tight-lipped expression of leery confusion. I liked making them squirm a bit. Made it all the more satisfying.

Some idiot yelled, "Play some Skynyrd!"

Never fails.

In the booth adjoining Rusty, another man sipped a whiskey sour he'd been nursing for the last hour and a half. He looked like the real straight-laced type, broad-shouldered, dressed in a white shirt and navy blue tie, his black blazer draped casually over the back of the booth. Basically the kind of guy you'd find in a big city bar, not this podunk metal-sided excuse for a nightclub. As soon as my eyes met his, he focused on his smartphone. It had been a recurring pattern all night. Something was up. Didn't matter. I had a mission, and I wasn't about to stop until I eliminated every nasty-ass redneck murderer who'd killed my mother.

I turned to the only temporary musician I could afford tonight, a doughboy bass guitarist with Willie Nelson braids named Keith.

"Every Breath You Take," I said.

"Huh? The Police song?"

"Yeah. Just follow along."

He shrugged. "You're the boss."

I always ended hunting nights with this song, whether the mark was in attendance or not. Very cliché, I know, but hey, it's a classic. It sounded especially haunting with a slow tempo and breathy lyrics. As I sang, Rusty got fidgety.

His phone buzzed again. He picked it up and stared at the screen, flicked his eyes toward me, and then texted something. His drunken red cheeks paled. The text probably read something like this: *Ted's dead. Lost his head. Get the hell out of there.* Or maybe his wife had sent him a picture of her cooter. I'm sure it would have had the same effect.

As I sang the final verses, Rusty took a wad of cash from his raggedy wallet with a trembling hand. He slapped the cash on the table with his receipt, eyes darting around like a nervous prey animal, and stood up.

The guy in the other booth stood, too, tossed some cash on the table, and slipped into his blazer. His eyes met mine once again, lingering a heartbeat longer than they should have. Then he headed for the door. I hoped he just thought I was super good-looking or super freaky. Otherwise, he could complicate things.

As I sang the last verse, Rusty went for the back exit. We wrapped up the song. People clapped and hollered. A fat, wannabe cowboy with a bolero and man nipples showing through his white shirt threw two twenties on the stage. I snatched them up, winked at him, and gave half to Keith.

I set the mike in the stand. "Be right back. Gotta hit the ladies' room."

"Okay. Uh..." Keith scratched his chest and averted his eyes.

That was one of the bad parts about not having your own band. Trust issues were inevitable.

"You'll get your forty percent of the cover. Just give me a sec, okay? I'll leave my guitar here as collateral."

"Thanks, Melody."

Cowboy Wannabe wasn't done with me apparently. He whistled. "Aw, come on, can't I at least see some titties? I'll throw in a hundred for a handy."

I stuck the twenty in my bra and gave him the middle finger.

"Dumb bitch!" He hurled his beer bottle at me. It hit my knee and splattered the cheap brew all over my skirt.

He would seriously regret that. My eye twitched. I stopped the bottle from rolling off the stage with my boot and stepped down on the glass until it shattered. He started laughing. I swooped down and grabbed him by the collar, lifting him until the toes of his boots barely touched the floor. He went dead quiet, his eyes as big as saucers.

I peered straight into them, letting the natural growl of my voice emerge as I whispered, "What's your name?"

"R-Ricky."

"Do you have a death wish, Ricky?"

"N-No, uh, I'm sorry."

"That's right. You're a real sorry excuse for a human."

"Wh-What are you?"

"Wanna find out?" My canines started to elongate, but then I realized this little exchange had attracted too many sets of eyes. The bouncer was headed toward us. I tossed Ricky on a table. "He's all yours."

"Yeah, okay, no problem," the bouncer said, hand hovering over the Taser on his belt.

Shit, I'd wasted too much time already. Trying to keep my pace at an acceptable speed, I ran down the back hall and out the back door. Standing still for a moment, I tried to catch Rusty's scent. Flies swarmed around the dumpster which stank of rotten potatoes, cigarette butts, and a confusing mess of human nastiness.

Letting my natural speed take over, I zipped out of the alley and into the parking lot of a nearby school, where I melted into the darkness behind a big poplar tree to avoid the security lights. I picked up Rusty's scent, but it was too faint to tell which direction he'd gone. I couldn't let him get away, not this time. Luckily, I'd been in disguise, but someone had tipped him off. It was only a matter of time before they discovered my true identity. Not that it mattered much. I had no family left to protect, nothing left to lose.

The squeal of metal sliding against metal drew my attention to the school's playground. Wind blew the swings haphazardly from side to side. Glancing around to ensure no one was watching, I dashed over to them and held the two cold chains of a swing in my hands, letting the rusted links press into my palms. Indulging my memory for a moment, I sat in the seat, closed my eyes, and pictured another time and place.

The moon spilled silvery light over a playground just like this in some other town. Mama and I both swung, higher and higher. I thought we might fly off into the starry sky if we got high enough. Our laughter mingled together like the harmony of birdsong at twilight. And in those moments, we were simply Bronwen and Wren. Mother and daughter. We loved playing outside, even on a frigid winter's night like that one. Snow crunched beneath our boots as we raced one another to the slide. The cold never bothered me. I complained about wearing a coat, but Mama had insisted.

"Wren, what will people think, if they see you with no coat? They'll know you're not human."

We ducked behind a snow drift when headlights illuminated the night. It was all a game back then.

"Stay out of sight," she said, "and if you can't, blend in. Be one of them. Never show anyone what you really are."

"What am I, Mama?"

I'll never forget how sparkling white her teeth were when she smiled. "You're special, my Wren, very special. One day you will know just how special you are."

As the memory faded, I swung higher and higher, until yellow light shone through my eyelids. My eyes popped open. Headlights, dissected by the hexagonal wire pattern of the chain-link fence, nearly blinded me. I squinted and gripped the swing chains so tightly they hurt as the truck barreled toward me.

I let my teeth fully emerge and stood up in the swing, which still swooped back and forth like a trapeze. Gun metal glinted in the security lights. Rusty popped off a shot as he raced by me on the road. The bullet clinked as it ricocheted off the swing set and cut a fiery streak across my ankle.

No time for a damage assessment. Using the momentum of the swing at its highest point, I launched myself straight at the truck and landed in the bed. I plunged my fist through the back glass and caught Rusty around the throat, nails digging in to get a good hold. He slammed on the brakes. But I held tight, bracing myself against the metal frame of the truck bed.

Rusty made a gurgling sound as the truck fishtailed and skidded to a jerky stop. I dragged him through the back glass and into the truck bed, crashing him down onto the floor. Crouching over him, I stared straight into his eyes, those same eyes that had flashed with wicked glee as he'd kicked my mother in the ribs and laughed as she writhed under the mesh of a silver net.

He stretched his hand in vain to reach the gun that had clattered into the truck bed with him. I knocked it away. That's when I noticed the tattoo on his arm - it looked like some kind of stick man with a diamond shaped body. Every single one of the killers had the same mark. It had to be some kind of gang symbol. Blood spurted from his neck where my nails had pierced his artery. It gurgled in his throat. He spat it out, straight into my face.

I laughed and licked my lips. "Hi, Rusty, remember me?"

His voice was bubbly and wet as he tried to speak. "Who are you?"

"I'm Wren. But you can call me Karma. She's a real bitch, isn't she?"

My fangs fully emerged. I plunged them into his neck and gulped down his blood as he keened pitifully like a deer caught in the jaws of a wolf. I drank until death throes wracked his body with involuntary spasms. I drank until my lips felt the last faint beat of his heart.

Sitting up, I closed my eyes and let my head fall back to relish the taste of another name crossed off my list. Then I swallowed down the final mouthful of thick, hot blood and let it settle in the pit of my stomach before wiping my mouth with my sleeve. Black clothes did a lot to hide a good night's meal.

The tiniest shuffling noise in the shadow of the poplar tree grabbed my attention. My eyes popped open, and I could smell him – the spicy cologne, a whiff of whiskey sour, new leather shoes.

In a flash, I zoomed in, being sure to crunch some gravel on the ground with my boot before I bounded up into the tree branches. Just as I expected, the well-dressed man from the bar rushed around the trunk and into the glow of the security lights, gun ready. He scanned the area quickly, and as soon as he turned and looked up, I grinned and pounced, knocking him onto his back. The gun went off and blew off a chunk of the concrete sign that read Silversage Elementary School.

I pinned down his arms as I straddled him. "Somebody brought the big guns, I see." My fangs emerged again.

When I dove in for his neck, he yelled, "Wait. I can help you!"

I paused just a hair's breadth from his racing pulse. He smelled even more interesting up close, like lemons and lavender. A smell I could savor for hours. Blinking myself back to reality, I raised my head and looked into his eyes. They were wide, full of fear, but also with an odd sense of finality, as though he were ready to die. As though he had nothing left to lose. Like me.

"What do you mean, you can help me?" I quickly glanced around us, making sure he hadn't brought reinforcements. We seemed to be all alone on the vacant schoolyard.

"You're looking for the ones who killed your mother, right? So am I."

I had to laugh at that. "Pray tell, why would you be looking for them, and why would you care..." Leaning in close, I added, "...human?"

"Detective Zac Palmer. I'm investigating a crime ring involving vampire clans. I think they're responsible for your mother's death. I'll need someone like you to help me get information."

I really had to laugh then. "What are you talking about? Vampire clans? There was my mother, and there's me. That's hardly a clan."

He raised an eyebrow, looking truly dumbfounded. "You don't know?"

"Know what? Are you telling me there are more like me? More...vampires?"

One side of his mouth slanted up in an amused grin. "Oh honey, did you really think you're the only one?"

CHAPTER TWO

ASHE

IT WAS WHILE STANDING in the elevator of a fancy hotel in the city of Brightwell, with blood trickling between my fingers onto the shiny wooden floor, that I truly realized the definition of Fucked. Capitalized, outlined in red, spotlighted, and placed on a pedestal—Fucked.

My streak of luck was continuing in the same vein as the past several minutes. Some practical joker had pressed almost all the buttons in the elevator so it would stop on every floor.

Hilarious.

Standing in one place was easier than descending the forty-eight floors of stairs, though, and after this next stop, I had six more until freedom. But with the stake wound in my side and the bloodbath I'd just walked away from, that first taste of freedom would likely be just as sour as my stomach, which rode too high in my throat.

The elevator door opened on a couple that had fused themselves together at the lips. The woman—hardly more than a girl—wore a blue-sequined dress that barely went past her hips, and the guy wore a business suit several sizes too big. A wall of perfume, alcohol, and the coppery sweet smell of type O blood followed them inside.

The door closed, and we started down to the next floor.

I pressed myself into the corner, covering the puddle of blood with my shiny black oxfords, so they wouldn't see my face or the blood streaming to the floor. Most of it was mine, at least I was pretty sure, but I wore a black tux, so who the hell really knew. It was hard to remember everything that had just happened, but the Fucked part of it had carved into the backs of my eyelids with vivid detail. Replaying again and again in case I needed a reminder.

Wrong. It had gone all wrong.

The door opened, and I smashed my thumb to the close button. It did, much too slowly.

The guy came up for air long enough to say, "Lobby."

"Uh-huh." I glanced at the five glowing buttons on the wall panel, thinking maybe it would be easier to roll myself down the stairs instead. But I'd been stabbed, and my good ol' speedy healing was taking its sweet-ass time. I'd wait for it to kick in, save my strength, and then haul balls...somewhere. A train station. Six feet under. Anywhere other than here.

"Lobby," he said again.

"Got it covered, man."

The guy wrenched away from his girl's mouth. "Lobby, put the fangs away, babe."

Wait. Lobby? The girl's name was Lobby?

"I smell vampire blood," she said to him, and then turned to me, her fangs bared over her red-painted bottom lip. She must have worn that all-day lipstick like Jessica wore. Otherwise, her boyfriend would be wearing it now.

The elevator opened again. I jabbed the close button. Again.

Well, there was no denying it since anyone of the vampire persuasion could smell it, but I thought I'd try anyway. "Oh, it's nothing. My girlfriend just got a little excited...I guess."

The doors finally closed, and we sank another floor lower.

The guy nodded, seeming to know exactly what I was talking about. Hell, I didn't know what I was talking about. The blood was streaming from my side, not my dick, but since I was still turned toward the corner, no one could see that.

"Been there, dude. Been. *There*." He snapped his jaws into his girl's face, and her fangs slipped back into her pouting mouth. "You headed out to buy her a pint to ward off her hunger so she can take you again, huh?"

"Yeah..." Sure. Whatever got him to shut up. I needed to think about my next few steps, not some nonexistent girlfriend biting my cock off. Or trying to gnaw her way through my side, for that matter.

The girl's tongue poked from her lips as she eyed me up and down. If a purr had an expression, that would be it. "I bet it was the tux."

"Hey, I have a tux, Loddy," the guy said.

Oh. Loddy, not Lobby. It was hard to hear over the roar of my conscience. How had it gone so wrong in that penthouse?

"Really?" She touched his chest and arched into him. "Well, I guess we know what me and my fangs will be doing when you wear it."

This was a riveting conversation, so much so that once the elevator doors began to close, I slipped through them to leave them to it. Without me.

Behind me, the guy whistled as the elevator began to close. "Man, she really got him good. Look at all that blood."

On the way to the stairs, I fished out my throw-away phone and typed out another quick text. *Staircase 1-3 too*. And then: *And a promotion to co-managers*.

They knew to be thorough yet discreet, even while cleaning up the bloodstains in a crowded elevator. They'd have to be speedy too. I trusted it would get done.

Silence met me when I burst through the staircase door. The stairs were empty. Thank you, Vampire Jesus. I swept down them as fast as I could, holding tight to my side. The leakage seemed less now. Apparently my vampire healing took its sweet time when the stake had broken through ribs and had cut through at least one lung. Just a tad more brutal than my usual paper cut. But I still had blood caked all over my hand, so I bunched my fingers up into my sleeve cuff as I opened the lobby door.

Now to get past hotel security before being spott—too late.

The old vampire in a tan uniform locked eyes with me from his high wooden desk to the left, a phone pressed to his ear.

Shit. My organs, long past their prime, curled inward on themselves under his flinty stare. In my research of the building, I thought I'd read that he was a retired Queen's Knight from the Northern Vampire Clan. He looked it, too, with his box-like haircut and so much chest that he had no neck.

I gave him a casual nod as I passed, all innocence and charm like my usual self, my ears picking up the voice on the other end of the line.

"...and then there was this swirl of different colors in all sorts of patterns, and then I walked inside of it. I woke up after that, fell back asleep, and the dream picked up after that. Am I going crazy?"

Yes. Seemed like the guard had been caught up in someone's long-winded dream description, also known as the fifth circle of hell. At least it sounded like he'd be there a while.

I pushed through the glass doors into the night before I could hear his reply, then cut to the right down the sidewalk, speeding my pace just slightly. Inside, I wanted to run. But where? Not to my apartment surrounded by nosy neighbors, at least not yet. I needed a change of clothes, a little more cash than I had in my wallet, and then out of this city, maybe out of the Southern Clan. For good.

A nondescript white van pulled up across the street, and Ben and Joe hopped out, my clean-up crew. And co-managers as of tonight. They wore tuxes as well, their cleaning equipment discreetly tucked away in their pockets. Their gazes skated right past me. Good men. Even better employees. They hadn't asked any questions about why I needed their cleaning services tonight.

The air smelled heavy, weighed down by violent-looking rainclouds. Taxis and limos lined both sides of the busy street, the city lights glistening on their polished surfaces. They'd take me anywhere, but they had cameras installed. Then again, so did the hotel. Unlike in books and movies, vampires actually showed up on cameras and in mirrors. It fucking sucked. I'd ridden downtown in a taxi, but it had dropped me off about seven blocks away in front of another hotel brimming with men in tuxes and fancy women draped on their arms.

Not my usual scene—none of this was, especially the blood on my hands—but I faked it until I made it. Just like I had my entire life.

I kept walking. Not two minutes after Ben and Joe had arrived, a police car took the corner about twenty feet ahead of me with a sharp turn. The sight of it kicked me in the gut and triggered an alarm through my head that sounded an awful lot like *Ruuuuuunnn!*

Its red and blue lights flashed, but it didn't sound its siren. It squealed to a stop behind me, right in front of the hotel I'd just exited, drawing the stares of the well-dressed pedestrians strolling past.

I knew exactly what the police would find inside. I sped my pace a little more.

Clothes, cash... Where to go?

A sign on top of a cab on the next block caught my eye. Of course. Lynch's Drugstore, the same one my sister worked at, whom, I might add, was part of the reason I was now booking it from that hotel.

Sirens wailed in the distance. A lot of them from the sound of it.

The drugstore was in the neighborhood, so I hurried while still giving off the vibe that I owned this whole street. That I hadn't done anything wrong.

Which I hadn't, I reminded myself, but that didn't change a damn thing.

Women vampires and their personal DBDs—designated blood donors, aka "humans"—turned to stare, their lustful eyes attempting to snag mine. Some men turned to look too. I was drawing attention to myself because of my face, my body, but it couldn't be helped. By the time they learned what I was walking away from, I'd be long gone.

From outside Lynch's Drugstore, I peered in, but I didn't see my sister behind the register. She was always working the nightshift, though, so I strode around to the far side of the building, hoping I'd catch her on her break. A fifteen minute one every four hours. Pretty good detail to know for someone who hadn't spoken to her in six years.

There she was, my older sister, age thirty-two in human years. She leaned against the wall, one leg bent so her foot rested flat against the bricks. She wore jeans and a red work shirt tied into a side knot at her waist. Her long blonde ponytail fell down her shoulder and partially hid her face while she attempted to light the cigarette plugged into her mouth.

"Well, good thing you're already dead, I guess," I told her, coming to a stop a few feet away.

The flame caught and she took a drag, then turned toward me with a flicker of surprise in her orangish eyes through the puff of smoke. "Ashe?"

"Yeah." I studied her then, seeing her once-broken nose gushing blood, the bruises on her face, all since healed. But it didn't stop the fury, just as sharp and consuming as it had been six years ago. I shook with it. I wanted to go to that hotel penthouse I'd just left all over again.

She must've sensed the direction of my thoughts because she bowed her head, the ponytail on her shoulder hiding her face again. "Why are you here?"

She should've known. Or at least suspected. But she gave no sign that she did.

"I need your help," I said. "Some money. A change of clothes if you got them."

She snapped her head up, her eyes peeling back my layers, a look she'd mastered years ago when she thought I was lying to her about eating the last blood popsicle. "Why? And why do I smell blood on you?"

"It's nothing."

"Bullshit, Ashe. What did you do?"

She didn't know. But the picture I had of her with that bastard vampire Devin was taken just days ago, even though I'd made her swear to never see him again after what he did to her. It was either never see him again, or I would end him right then and there. That was the choice I'd given her, because I'd so badly wanted to hurt him as badly as he'd hurt her.

"Did you cut your hair?" I demanded, my voice as sharp as an accusation.

She took another drag of her cigarette, eyeing me closely.

A siren wailed in the distance, far away yet much too close.

"Maybe you've splashed around in one too many cleaning chemicals for your company," she said. "What's your cleaning business called again?"

"Invite Us In Cleaners," I said through gritted teeth. "Your hair, Jessica."

"No, I didn't cut my hair."

But...she had. The photo I'd seen was of her—with him—but with longer hair. Was she lying to me? If she'd met with Devin six years after my threat on his life, I supposed she was capable of it. But if I told her anything, then I'd have to tell her all of it, and I didn't know how to do that since I didn't know everything myself. For at least the fifth time tonight, my head felt like it might explode.

A crack of thunder shook the ground, drowning out the siren, but still urging me to hurry.

"Invite Us In." Jessica shook her head while lightning split across the sky. "Why not Spic n' Fang Cleaners?"

"Jessica—"

"Type A+ Cleaners and then in parenthesis"—she punched the air with her cigarette in an arc—"But We Like Other Blood Types Too?"

"Damn it, no—"

"I could've come up with something way better." She laughed. "We'll Lick Your Walls For You Cleaners."

"He's dead." I said it in a way that snapped each sound between us and then seemed to bulldoze their meaning into her all at once.

Her color, already at a bare minimum, washed from her face. She sagged against the wall, a puddle with bones.

"You?" Hardly a whisper.

I squeezed my eyes shut. She didn't know. Somehow, she didn't know that she'd been in a picture with Devin taken a few days ago, staring right at him and smiling. Now, she looked older than she did that night he'd beat her. Not older physically, but something had shifted behind her eyes. A hardness that hadn't been in that picture, but was here now, six years later.

That hadn't been her in the picture. Or somehow it was her and she didn't remember? The photo had the date printed right at the bottom.

It made no sense, but I didn't have time to unravel it right then.

I opened my eyes again. "I just need some clothes and some money. I'll pay you back."

She fished out her keys from her jeans pocket and chucked them at my head. I caught them midair, having had a lot of practice from childhood when she got pissed at me.

"Good," she said, her voice full of bite and then looked away, dismissing me. "Money's in a plastic bag taped to the inside of the toilet tank. Edgar may or may not let you leave with it."

Fair enough. Edgar was her pet iguana she'd had for twelve years. I backed away. My time here was done.

Jessica's apartment building was nearby, right over the line in a street a few blocks down that separated the tuxedo part of Brightwell from the slums. Her building couldn't decide what color it wanted to be, its gray and white and yellow and tan foundation easy to spot in the darkening night. She lived on the ground floor with window planters at each of her windows filled with bright flowers and a welcome mat outside her front door when no one else had one.

I let myself in and quickly locked the door behind me. It was dark inside, the sheer curtains drawn. It smelled warm and clean, not like my apartment a few blocks down. I cleaned at work, not at home.

I made my way through the living room to the hall-way, noting the framed, life-like drawings she'd done sitting on the bookshelves and lamp tables along the way. Our parents, long since moved to the Northern Vampire Clan, one of me in my Night League baseball uniform, another of me flipping her off.

Even though it had seemed she'd pushed me away these last six years without a single word, seeing these drawings felt like a kick to the chest. Before that night six years ago, we'd never been particularly close since we didn't have much in common. I never knew she'd done drawings of me, so I must've annoyed her enough to make some kind of impression. Not going to lie—it felt good.

A faint scratching sounded from somewhere on my way down the hallway. Edgar, probably. I found the money in the toilet tank, taking only what I thought I would need, washed the dried blood from my hands, then strode toward Jessica's closet in her bedroom. Of course we weren't the same size, but as long as I could fit into a shirt and sweatpants or something, I'd make do. Hell, I'd even settle for something pink or lacy.

I was relieved when I didn't have to.

After I changed into oversized sweatpants and a gray Brightwell East High P.E. Dept. shirt, I found a bag to stuff my bloodied tux in and then hurried back down the hallway.

More scratching came, almost like a rustling in a distinct, rhythmic pattern.

My steps toward the front door slowed, my flesh slinking back the way I came.

I knew that sound. Not Edgar. Not raindrops. Not yet.

Footsteps through dead grass right outside the sheer-curtained living room window.

No. *No*.

I dropped to the ground right before a white spotlight as bright and shocking as the sun blasted through the window. Seconds later, the front door burst open. Voices shouted at me to do fifty things at once.

Fucked. Capitalized, outlined in red, literally spotlighted, and placed on a pedestal—Fucked.

Had Jessica called the police on me? Had she been lying and that really *had* been her in the photo with Devin?

"Hands in the air where I can see them!"

Because she only knew half the story.

"Now!"

Yes, I'd gone to the hotel to kill him.

But he was already dead.

CHAPTER THREE

WREN

THE DETECTIVE STARED AT me like I'd grown an extra set of fangs on my chin. "Did your mother tell you nothing?"

"She told me..." I still had him pinned down, but damn it, he was actually good-looking. Think Henry Cavill as Superman hot, except for a somewhat crooked nose that had probably been broken a time or two. Still...definitely not my usual reeks-of-body-odor prey. "This is ridiculous. You're trying to mess with my head. We're done here."

Fangs bared, I leaned in and pricked the skin of his neck.

He was eerily still. No struggle. No tensed muscles.

Damn it to hell and back. I couldn't fucking do it. I sat up straight, slowly releasing his arms but still straddling him. He felt solid and warm beneath my hips and between my legs. I could already imagine how that warmth might feel inside me.

Then the weight of what he had said dropped on me and pushed those sexy thoughts aside. I wasn't the only one. Wracking my brain, I tried to remember if my mother had said anything at all about other vampires. I'd asked about my father once. She said he died and it was best to not talk about him. So I didn't. But now I wish I had drilled her more, made her tell me something, *anything*, about what we were and where we came from.

But she'd died before I'd had a chance.

"Shit." I sprang off him and to my feet, licking a tiny droplet of his blood from my fang. It tasted a whole lot better than Rusty's cholesterol-thickened sludge. Like a meal from a restaurant I couldn't afford.

He slowly sat up, holstered his gun, and eased himself to his feet while I kept a couple yards between us. "She never told you there were other vampires?"

"The only thing she told me is that I had a father, and he died. I was eight fucking years old, okay? I didn't know enough to know what I *should* have asked her."

He scratched his head. I'd probably confused him with my own confusion, but hey, at least we were on the same playing field.

"But you never thought there might be more of...your kind?"

"Sure, it's occurred to me since then, but none have made themselves known, and I haven't gone looking for them. When she died, I was a little busy keeping myself fed so I could grow strong enough to track her murderers down and rip their throats out."

"What did you plan to do when you accomplished that?"

"Oh, I don't know, anything from stabbing myself with a wooden stake to falling into a volcano. Why the hell do you care?"

"I can't tell you anything here."

"Listen closely, Detective Zac Palmer. If you're pulling something, I swear I will rip out your guts and strangle you with them before I drain you dry. Is that clear?"

"Yes, ma'am. Couldn't be clearer."

"Start talking. How did you find me, and how do you know about my mother?"

He glanced around, then shook his head. "Not here."

"Okay, then where?"

"We'll have to take a little road trip."

"A road trip. To where? Disney World?"

"Yeah, uh, no. There's a little town called Brightwell. I want to find a certain vampire there."

"A *certain* vampire. Do we have a name for this vampire?"

"No."

"Okay. A specific location?"

"No."

I crossed my arms. "Wow, that's a lot to go on, *Detective*. You just show up out of the blue, interrupt my dinner, and tell me you want to help me. You don't even know me. I could have killed you already. I still might if you keep annoying me. I mean, what the fuck?"

Did he know I didn't just kill random humans? I wasn't a mindless bloodsucker like some of the movies suggested.

"I admit I thought you'd know at least something about your kind," he said with a shrug, "but that doesn't matter. You'll be able to find him."

"Look, I'm pretty good at tracking if I have a scent or address or something to go on but..."

He approached. I backed away.

"It's okay. I'm not going to hurt you." He reached into his blazer, slowly.

I kept my eyes glued to his hand, ready to breeze on out of there if he produced a weapon. Instead, he pulled out what looked like a small flashlight and came close to me.

He glanced down at my arm. "Could you pull up your sleeve?"

Okay, that was random. "Why?"

"We don't have time for questions."

"Well, I don't have time for human assholery right now. Tell me what it's for."

He glanced around us, then whispered, "I think you have a mark that you probably have never seen. I think it's the key to this whole thing. This black light should reveal it."

"The key to what whole thing? I call bullshit, but fine. I'll play along." My eyes never left his hands as I drew my sleeve up, exposing my forearm. I turned it over, showing him all sides, including the rose vine tattoo that climbed all the way to my shoulder. "Just an arm."

He flicked on the flashlight. It had a strange purplish light. "Hold your arm out, wrist up."

I did what he asked, but this was getting old real fast. "Can we hurry this up? I still need to get my money and guitar back at the bar, and I've been in the 'ladies' room' way too long."

"Don't worry, I'll get your guitar back. The light will sting a little, but it's only UVA, so it won't hurt you, okay?"

I nodded, planting my feet just in case I needed to make a quick exit. "And my money?"

He smiled. "Yes, that too." Damn him, he could have doubled as Clark Kent. He shined the light on my forearm just below my wrist. I winced. It stung like an electric shock, but I didn't move. My skin started to glow pink, and as I watched, a bright pink circle blazed to life on my skin. It started to burn, so I yanked my arm back. In the blink of an eye, the circle had vanished.

"Shit, did you just mark me or something?"

"No," he said, chuckling. "Your mother probably did. Or your father, but that's how we'll find the vampire we need."

"What do you mean?"

"You'll see." He turned and started walking. "Let's go."

He wanted me to go on a road trip with him after pointing out the 'key to the whole thing' on my wrist. I still had no idea what he was talking about, but he knew my mother. Or knew something about her at least. Maybe he could help me track down the rest of her killers. Of course, road-tripping with strangers was how someone usually wound up dead. I'd just have to make sure it was him if he tried anything stupid.

I trailed after him. "Fine, but we're taking *my* car, and *you're* getting my guitar back."

WE DROVE ALL NIGHT, or I did anyway, hauling ass out of Silversage as Zac slept in the passenger seat. It was more than a little awkward, me driving my '59 Thunderbird (aka Birdie) six hours to Brightwell, Louisiana with a human I'd never met and didn't plan on eating, though that was still an option as far as I was concerned. His smell was enticing. Like a freshly mowed lawn and licorice spice drops or some shit like that. I'd have been content just licking on him like a human lollipop if he'd let me.

At the Alabama state line, we visited a near-empty truck stop where I used one of the trucker's showers to wash the last traces of blood off me. I also took off that itchy-ass wig and flushed it. I never wore the same wig twice. When I emerged, dressed in a gray hoodie and black leggings, Zac was waiting outside the bathroom. He did a double take.

"Wow. Another disguise?" He held a large coffee and a bag of donuts, and had traded his suit for a Mets T-shirt and jeans.

"Nope, just me, except the contacts."

"Suits you. The hair, I mean."

I shrugged. My natural hair was platinum blonde, nearly white like my mother's, and cut to a very short style that let me wash it, swipe some gel through it, and forget about it. Definitely natural enough to pass as human. My eye color, on the other hand, was a bright yellow, ringed with orange. Definitely *not* natural enough to pass as human. So, the designer contacts were a must.

We got back into the car, where Zac opened the bag of donuts and held one out to me. "Oh, sorry, I guess you don't eat those."

"Sure I can, but just a bite."

Zac pinched me off a piece. I popped it in my mouth, savoring the greasy, glazed goodness. The inevitable nausea came with it, but I respected my limits.

"What happens if you eat more?"

"Nothing much, just projectile vomiting."

"Oh." He stuck the rest of the donut back in the bag and folded the top closed before setting it in the floorboard.

"So what about you?" It was a long drive, and I still didn't know a whole lot about Zac Palmer except that he had a nice chin dimple and apparently got his rocks off studying vampires.

"I can eat just about anything. Not too fond of blood, though. My steaks have to be extra well done."

I huffed a laugh. "Sounds chewy. No, I meant what about you on a personal level? I imagine you have a wife and two point five brats somewhere in an immaculate suburb."

He exhaled through pursed lips, propping his elbow on the car door while he rubbed his temple. "No. I had a wife." He paused, jaw tightening as though it pained him to talk about his family. Well, that made two of us. "She died."

"Oh. How did –?"

"Car wreck." He zipped up his jacket and scrunched himself up against the door, eyes closed. "I'm going to catch a few more Zs so I'll be ready to get to work once we get there."

"Okay." So that was the end of the *All About Zac* show, apparently, as unsatisfying as a quick fuck with a trucker who wouldn't pay up after. Maybe I could get more out of him if I ... *No, bad Wren!*

I let him sleep as I drove another couple hours along Interstate 12 in Louisiana until the sun oranged the line between earth and sky. I'd never seen a full sunrise. I always wondered what humans felt when that big ball of hot light popped over the horizon. Does it take your breath away? Bring tears to your eyes? Make you grateful for life, for the steady beat of your heart, the warm blood flowing through your veins?

Waking up with a stretch and yawn, Zac looked at me, then out the window. "It's beautiful when it rises, especially over the ocean."

"I wouldn't know." Our destination was only a mile or so off the Gulf Coast, somewhere between Baton Rouge and New Orleans. "Maybe if I wore SPF three thousand, a burka, and sunglasses, I could watch it."

"Don't worry. We'll be there in just a minute, so we should be able to avoid it. What's it like, though, if you're in the sun? Do you sparkle?" There was a hint of a smile in his voice, but I didn't share his amusement.

"I don't fucking sparkle. Me and the sun don't get along too well."

"How so?" He sat there blinking at me, waiting for an explanation.

Frowning, I swallowed hard, still tasting Rusty's nasty blood on the back of my throat. It wasn't really fair to expect me to do all the talking, while he offered nothing about himself beyond a penchant for vampires and a dead wife.

But his curious puppy-dog eyes and chin dimple were annoyingly persuasive. Was that some human super-power I didn't know about?

Fine. I hated uncomfortable silences. "I don't immediately burst into flames or anything that dramatic. It's more like a severe sun allergy, like those creepy little kids in that movie, *The Others*, only amplified. A little bit isn't going to kill me, but I'll end up with an annoying rash at best and second- or third-degree burns if I'm in the sun longer than ten or twenty seconds. Longer than that, and my skin will basically slough off, followed by the rest of me, until I'm a pile of ashes. Or so my mother told me, one of only a few useful bits of information she volunteered that helped me survive this long."

"I'm sorry she didn't tell you more."

"Yeah, me too."

"How did you two survive alone? Did you go to night school?"

"School? Oh yeah, I went to school, wore a uniform and everything. Came home every day to fresh chocolate chip cookies right from the oven."

"Really?"

I smirked at him. "No, not really. I fell asleep in nasty basements and woke up in nastier motel rooms. Mama taught me to read and do basic math. Sometimes we were lucky enough to get a working TV so I could watch the History Channel or some cheesy-ass vampire movie. But mostly, I learned to hide and hunt and how to never get too attached to any place...or anyone."

Quiet followed. I squirmed in the driver's seat, suddenly aware of how stiff and cold and dead I was compared to him. He stared straight ahead out the windshield, glancing at me a couple times before consulting his phone.

"Up here," he said, consulting his smart phone. "There's a hotel downtown. Take exit five."

"Okay." A half mile before the exit, I had to ask for the fiftieth time. "Why are you doing this? How do I know you're not leading me into a trap?"

"I guess you don't, but how do I know you aren't leading *me* into one? You could have easily killed me last night. Or while I slept."

He had a point, I guess. I could definitely still kill him, though it would be a shame to not enjoy his pretty face for a while longer. Plus, my curiosity was overwhelming at this point. I hadn't studied my heritage, though those questions had lingered in the back of my mind over the years I'd spent tracking down those who had killed my mother.

"Who is this vampire you're looking for?" I asked. "Is he related to me?"

"I'm not really sure, to be honest. I had a lead on his location, and that somehow he is connected to you and Bronwen."

"But why do you care? What are my mother and I to you?"

He was silent for a moment, rubbing his chin and the five o' clock shadow that had darkened his face overnight. "An assignment," he said with a note of finality. "I need to find out just how interconnected the vampire clans are, and how the social hierarchy works among them."

"Sounds very scholarly. But why do you need to know this?"

"We believe vampires are contributing to corruption of human politics."

"Since when do humans need help with corruption?"

He chuckled. "True enough. But those of us who care want to fight it in any way we can."

"You want to fight vampires?" His intentions were still murky to me, but at least he was talking. How much of it consisted of truth rather than lies, I didn't know, but it did help pass the time.

"Not exactly. We don't know how deep their associations are with the powers that be. But there have been assassinations on both sides that lead us to believe they're a lot more connected than they appear. And if they go far enough up the political ladder, we could have a war on our hands."

"Assassinations?" I swallowed past the mental picture of my mother's severed head that had wedged its way into the forefront of my thoughts. "Like my mother's, you mean?"

"Yes, and others."

"What do you know so far?"

He inhaled deeply and rubbed his eyes, blinking the sleep from them. "There are four clans divided among the continental US. I know your mother was someone of importance to the Southern Clan, and that she went missing about twenty-five years ago before turning up dead seventeen years ago."

My mind flipped through all the times we had traded one town for another, sheltered in cellars, abandoned houses, and asylums, where spirits lurked in the edges of the shadows while we slept, curious about the pale, blood-supping creatures who seemed even deader than they were. Little did I know that she'd been hiding that whole time, from someone or maybe several someones who wanted her dead.

"She was important how?" I asked, finally escaping from the restraints of my memories.

"I'm not sure, except that she was some sort of leader." He paused, his gaze flicking to me before he focused on the road ahead. "There was some talk of her having a child. But I'm not sure how many knew about you or the details. It was hard enough for *me* to track you down since I'm just a lowly human, but I took a chance and banked on the rumors being true."

Exit five loomed ahead, so I merged onto the off-ramp. "How *did* you track me down?"

"Just followed the body trail. You've been pretty efficient in killing known lowlifes, all of them in the same fashion, throats ripped open, blood drained."

"You're welcome."

He grinned. "Turn right at the stop light."

I did as directed, then drove through another mile of boring farmland until we reached an urban area that resembled those of many small cities in the south. The historic district made up the town's heart, but with all the new paint, paving, signage, and LED 'gaslights,' one could argue the validity of its true historic worth.

"Here, we can get a room." Zac gestured to a hotel sign – *Hotel Enigma* – that jutted over the sidewalk to the left.

"We?"

"I mean you. I'll get *you* a room since I assume you're not a fan of the sun, and I can gather a little more information while you sleep."

"If you insist." I turned into the small parking garage, which was tricky with a not-at-all-compact '59 Thunderbird.

"For a vampire who's in hiding, don't you think you should drive something a little smaller and less…" He waved his hand around as though he didn't know how to finish that insult to my preferred transportation method.

"Less what? Awesome? I don't think anyone will expect a vampire to be driving a classic like this."

"Hiding in plain sight? Like your Melody Songsmith persona?"

"Something like that." I found a parking spot and hurried out of the car, then grabbed my backpack and guitar from the back seat as the sun popped between buildings and blazed over the concrete wall of the garage. It felt like the burning rush of heat from opening a convection oven.

I zipped inside through the glass door that led to the lobby. Zac followed a few seconds later carrying a small duffel bag of his own. Hotel Enigma's air conditioning quickly cooled my heated skin, except for one spot on my arm, the same spot that Zac had uncovered with his UV light. It didn't really burn so much as tingle, like an electric buzz. I pulled up my sleeve and stared at the faintly glowing circle.

Zac wrapped his hand over it and shook his head. I took that as a sign that this wasn't a brag-worthy tattoo like the rest I had. A custodian came by with a dust broom and nodded at us, but his gaze lingered on me as he passed. I pulled down my sleeve.

"Come on," Zac whispered, and I followed him to the front desk. He flashed a Clark Kent smile at the older black woman working behind the front desk.

Her name tag read *Karen, General Manager.* "Good morning. Checking out?"

"No, checking in, actually. My wife and I have been driving all night. I hope you have a room available."

"Oh sure, honey. All I need is a credit card and your driver's license."

Though I pretended to be browsing the tourist brochures advertising petting zoos, canoeing, and civil war reenactments, I could feel Karen's eyes on me. Was I glowing all over or something? Maybe it was my nose ring. She seemed like the Sunday-school-teacher type, not the nose-ring-and-tattoo type.

A couple minutes later, key card in hand, we rode up the elevator to the fourth floor and got off. A whiff of something hit me – like blood, but...dead blood. Like my mother's had smelled the night she died. I froze in the hallway.

"Come on," Zac whispered.

I followed him to room 410, where he scanned up and down the hallway before opening the door. We quickly slipped inside. Sunlight blinded me, so I ducked into the tiny bathroom. He locked both the deadlock and chain lock, then ran to the curtains and drew them. Once the sunlight had been drowned out, I emerged and sat on one of the queen beds. The flowery bedspread wafted up scents of human bodily fluids, so I tore off the bedspread and flopped down on the bleached sheets. It wasn't like I'd die of gonorrhea or something, but...ew.

"What did you experience out there? Feelings? Smells?"

"I smelled blood, but I don't think it was human."

"Vampire?"

"Maybe. It was kind of faint. But this…" I pulled up my sleeve and showed him the lightly glowing circle on my forearm. "It seems to be pulsing, actually. And it's tingling, like a small electrical charge."

I sat up, staring at the faint pink marking. Zac came over with the UV light and shined it on my arm again. The sting made me wince, but I held still. Adjacent to the first marking was a very faint blue diamond shape, one end of it touching the pink circle.

He turned off the light and nodded. "Perfect."

"What is it though? What does it mean?"

"It means we're close. He's probably been here."

"The vampire we're looking for?"

"Exactly."

"And how will we find him?"

"Just follow the yellow brick road," he said, pointing at my arm.

I SLEPT THROUGH THE day, cocooned in the sheets and blanket. The only sounds that disturbed me were a few slamming doors, a jackhammer somewhere on the sidewalk below, sirens, and a car alarm.

Zac slept a couple hours in the other bed, then spent the rest of the day "gathering information," whatever that meant. He returned as I was waking just after sundown and knocked five times - our chosen signal. I looked through the peephole just to be sure. He stood there with a bag of fast food, waving. I opened the door and stood aside to let him in.

"Sleep well?" he asked.

"Like the dead." I stretched and grinned up at him, fangs and all.

He laughed nervously as he went to the desk and deposited the food. "Nice eyes."

"Oh, yeah, sorry." I'd taken out my contacts because they annoyed the shit out of me when I slept. "What did you find?"

"We need to head to the east end of town. There's a jail there."

"A jail? Is this guy a criminal?"

"Allegedly."

Time for another round of let's extract one-word answers from Zac. "And what exactly did he do to land himself in jail?"

Zac hesitated, slowly removing his burger from the bag. "Murder."

A cold shiver ran through me. *Rabbit ran over my grave*, Mama used to say. "And who did he murder?"

"Allegedly murdered."

"Okay, who did this mystery vampire allegedly murder?"

"I'm not totally sure until I get more information. He may be innocent for all I know."

I couldn't tell if he was hiding anything. His expression was set in stone. His heartbeat maintained a clock-like rhythm. "And what business do we have visiting an *alleged* murderer in jail?"

"We need him, and I don't think he's dangerous."

"Well, if you say so..." I rolled my eyes. "But if he goes berserk on your ass, don't come crawling to me. Address?"

"That I don't know exactly. I'll need you for that. We'll roll out of here a little closer to dawn."

"Why wait?"

"Don't worry. I have a plan."

"Of course you do." I rubbed my arm, which still tingled. It hadn't let up, but the sensation had an odd calming effect on me, almost like I'd felt with my mother – safe and at home.

"I'll hop in the shower while you gnaw on your hamburger." I had to bite my tongue to keep from adding, *Wanna join me?* Had I fully trusted him, I'd have no problem riding him for a few hours. No way would I make myself that vulnerable. But...how long had it been since I'd had a good fuck? I honestly couldn't remember.

****

"Sure you don't want me to drive?" Zac asked as we got in the car.

"Quite sure, thank you. Nobody drives my car but me."

"Okay, but you'll have to pay attention to the mark on your arm so we know when we're getting close."

"It's a game of vampire Marco Polo. I got this."

"If you say so. Let's head east on Market and get on the bypass."

Maybe the sleep and shower had made me overconfident. But I felt pretty awesome in my clean black leggings, black army boots, and black tank top. I skipped the wig, but I wore a fresh pair of green contacts so I wouldn't totally freak people out.

In the dim car interior, it was easy to see the magic tattoo glowing on my arm. The farther we drove, the brighter the blue diamond became, and the faster the light pulsed.

A weird sense of urgency kept my eyes wide and scanning the road ahead. "If this is a jail, wouldn't it be closer to town? Or are we talking state pen or insane asylum?"

"No, I don't think this one is known to the general public."

We went through an intersection on the near-vacant bypass. The sensation lessened. I hit the brakes and did a sudden U-turn, tires squealing on the damp pavement of a humid Louisiana summer.

Zac grabbed the "oh shit" handle as he slammed against the passenger door. "What the –!"

"Wrong way." I turned left down a narrow highway with no road sign on the metal sign post. The symbol on my arm grew brighter and buzzed like a tattoo pen on high speed. "This way."

I stomped the gas, concentrated on shifting gears to keep Birdie growling along the curvy, pothole-scarred highway. Tree limbs draped with Spanish moss hung low overhead. They smacked the windshield as though warning us to go back the way we came.

I couldn't stop then even if I wanted to. No clue where we were headed, but I knew we had to get there. Up ahead on the right was a scattering of gravel and an opening in the trees. The buzzing on my arm grew almost unbearable, so I stomped the brakes again and pulled just off the highway.

A small gravel road snaked off through the darkness. There were no signs, but a few lights flickered in the distance. I got out of the car, as did Zac, who still looked shaken up from the wild ride.

"So," he said quietly, "I take it we've found him."

"Maybe." I allowed my night vision to light up the dark forested road, detecting both shapes and temperatures. Yellow human shapes moved in the distance, each holding cooler lines the shape of what else? Guns.

"This is no ordinary jail, is it?" I whispered.

"No." Zac racked the slide of his gun. "You feel like he's in there?"

"Oh, yeah." And then a name wiggled its way into my thoughts. "Ashe. His name is Ashe."

CHAPTER FOUR

ASHE

ACCORDING TO THE INFORMATION scribbled on the graffitied desk I sat in front of, Detective Nuyen liked ball. Just one, apparently. That had been written in black ink along the edge, and then carved all through it were the letters A-S-K over and over.

Nah. I was in enough trouble without asking, but I traced the message again and again, avoiding looking up from it. Every time I did, the walls pressed in and threatened to crush me into nothing but blood and bone and just as Fucked as I was now.

I'd never had the pleasure of seeing the inside of a human jail before, but I imagined it was a lot like this vampire-proof one. Peeling paint along the walls, tile floors that were so uneven they'd make you face-plant every two steps if you weren't careful, and reeking of desperation and someone's spoiled leftovers in the corner trash. I imagined the only differences were the pure silver doors and heavy window coverings that blocked out all light.

Well, almost all light.

I rubbed the red singe mark on my arm that had only just stopped sizzling a few hours ago. A smug officer had led me right through the thin shaft of light slanting through on the way to this room and didn't appear to give two fucks about my little sun allergy.

The door to the interview room burst open, and in walked a tall, husky vampire with hardly any eyebrows and even less hair on his head. He wore a blue suit, tie, and matching gloves with which to latch the silver door. His yellow eyes flashed when he turned them on me, tilted upward and cat-like.

Detective Nuyen, I guessed, and no, he didn't like ball. Sometimes you can just tell, no asking required.

"Ashe Jensen," he barked and slapped down a tan file folder on the table in front of me.

I wished I could be literally anyone else. My stomach shifted at how badly I wished that, and at how empty it had become. I was used to looking and acting like I belonged anywhere, faking it until I made it, but here? I had to get out.

"No. Sorry," I said. "Try next door?"

Not even a crack as he settled himself in the metal chair across from me. It was worth a shot.

"Your attorney, Mr. Phillips, is on his way," he said.

I didn't have an attorney, not one I could afford anyway, so one had been provided for me. I imagined the worst.

A knock sounded on the door, then an officer let in a madman in a brown suit, his white hair flying in all directions behind him. He clutched his briefcase to his chest like it contained the last fresh blood supply in the world, and judging from the way his yellow eyes bugged, I would bet he hadn't blinked in years. And his fly was undone.

Yep. Worst. I was so screwed.

"Have you said anything?" he demanded.

"Not—"

"Don't!"

I didn't.

He poured himself into the chair next to mine, dropping his briefcase to the floor. What sounded like glass bottles rattled from the inside. Either it really was the last fresh blood supply in the world, or my lawyer had brought his own bar.

"Now then," Detective Nuyen said. "Let's talk about what happened last night."

"These are outrageous charges." Mr. Phillips fished out a notebook and pen from inside his jacket, then leaned toward me with a lowered voice. "Did you do it?"

"No."

"That makes my job a hell of a lot easier." He readied himself to take notes on what I was about to say.

The problem was I didn't know where to begin, or how much the police already knew. One of them had mentioned a search warrant of my apartment, but there was nothing there that linked me to Devin. The fact that I'd been sitting here for hours stewing in my own guilt even though I hadn't done anything obviously wasn't a good sign, but I hadn't done anything wrong. If I could spin my story to where I hadn't even *thought* about doing something wrong, then maybe there was some small chance I could walk out of here. Someday. Eventually.

Detective Nuyen looked at me closely, the fluorescents above his bald head filling the natural dips of his skull. "Where were you between the hours of nine o'clock and midnight last night?"

"Don't answer that," Mr. Phillips ordered.

Not answering made me look guilty, and I wasn't. Not really. I shifted in my chair and shuffled my silver-chained feet, my chest feeling too tight like I'd forgotten to draw a breath for the last thirty years. The police had found my bloodied tux in the plastic bag at my sister's apartment and had likely seen my face on the security cameras at the hotel, so there was no sense in lying about that part. I just had to spin it right.

"I was at a party with about fifty other people," I said. "At Hotel Enigma's penthouse."

"Who were you invited by?" Detective Nuyen asked.

Mr. Phillips clicked his pen as fast as I fidgeted my feet. "You don't have to answer."

I shrugged. "A friend of a friend."

"Had you met Devin Tallerson, the owner of the penthouse, before?" the detective asked.

At hearing his name, fury from that night six years ago blasted through me once again, squeezing my fists into tight balls. He had broken Jessica's nose so it sat crooked on her face before her vampire healing had kicked in. How could anyone do that, especially to my sister? Despite her being older and tougher, my sister was still a breakable, little thing.

Mr. Phillips shook his head at me, a warning.

"Yes," I grinded out. "I knew him."

"Were you aware that Devin practiced mithridatism?"

Mr. Phillips rocked back into his chair, his jaw lying in his lap. The pen flew from his fingers and dropped at my chained feet.

My skin prickled as I glanced between the two of them. Mithridatism? I shook my head. "I don't even know what that is."

Detective Nuyen's yellow eyes fixed on me, reading every movement as I bent to retrieve Mr. Phillips's pen. "Over the years, Devin poisoned himself daily in small, non-lethal doses of silver and holy water to protect himself, to become immune to their effects."

His words shocked over me like a deep, arctic wave. No. No, I hadn't known that. How would I? If I had known, I wouldn't have planned on killing him with the vial of pure liquid silver I'd dumped into his glass of blood in his bedroom. He'd never had a chance to drink it.

"Who would do something like that?" I asked.

Detective Nuyen leaned forward. "Someone who thought others were out to get him."

There had been others, and not just me. You couldn't shoot yourself through the heart in small, non-lethal doses to become immune to it, and that was how I'd found him. What was left of him anyway since he'd been a pile of goo. I'd found the silver shell casing. So who else had wanted him dead? And why?

"The experts say that mithridatism can change people the longer it's utilized, make them even more paranoid and increasingly violent over the years." The detective brought out a picture from the tan file folder and placed it in front of me. "His paranoia may be what caused him to change his appearance, too."

I glanced down at the picture of a man, a man who looked nothing like Devin. Different hair, different eyes, different eye *shape*. Who the hell was this?

"That picture was taken close to ten years ago when Devin Tallerson was hiding out and went by a different name," the detective said. "Did you ever hear of any episodes where Devin became violent or paranoid?"

So much blood all over my sister's face. It mixed with her tears and dribbled down on her fuzzy slippers she wore around her apartment, once white like snowballs, and then crimson.

I shook my head, unable to push out a sound around that memory.

"You own a cleaning service called Invite Us In Cleaners and clean up crime scenes on occasion. Is that correct?" Detective Nuyen asked.

My lawyer looked at me, the doubt in his wide eyes scratching at the inside of my skull. "Don't say a word."

But it was too late for that, wasn't it? The detective already knew. I closed my eyes briefly because I knew exactly how this must look. Murder someone and then use my expertise to clean up thoroughly so no one could tell I'd had anything to do with it. But I hadn't had time to clean up. I'd been too busy getting staked in the lung after I discovered Devin already dead.

The detective ruffled the corner of the folder, a smug smile flashing across his predatory features as if he were cleaning the bird meat from his teeth with one of its bones. "That was quite a bloodstain on your tux we found. What happened there?"

Beyond being stuck at the wrong end of a stake—wielded by a phantom as far as I was concerned—I understood absolutely nothing about that part of my fucked-up night.

My lawyer shook his head and sighed.

Detective Nuyen opened the tan file folder between us and handed Mr. Phillips a paper. "This is the warrant used to search your client's apartment." He pushed several photos from the file toward me. "Is this your apartment?"

Stained carpet, piles of wadded-up clothes thrown in the corners, stacks of mail teetering on my coffee table. Yes, it was my apartment, but... My eyes widened as I stared closer at one of the photos.

"What's that coming out of the bottom of the coffee table?" I asked. It looked like the corner of a holey blanket. Big holes in a pattern shaped like diamonds.

No, not a blanket at all. A silver net I'd never seen before.

A knock sounded at the door, and the detective rose to answer it. "You tell me, Ashe. It's your apartment, isn't it?"

"Don't say a word more," my lawyer muttered.

The officer outside handed the detective another folder, this one white.

As he strode back to the table, I looked at him straight-on so he could see I was telling him the truth. "That's not mine. Someone put that there. I don't own any nets."

Without sitting, he opened the new folder, his gaze pinned to me. "So you do know what it is."

He had to be shitting me, or trying to trick me into some kind of confession. Just not the crime I'd been accused of.

I threw my hands up and sat back in the chair. "I know what it is because I just looked at the goddamn picture you showed me."

"Do you know whose blood is on it?" he asked and waved the white folder in his hands. "I have the report right here."

"Blood? No." What the hell were we even talking about now? We'd gone from poisoning to bloody nets, and I had no clue why. "Look, I didn't kill anyone. There were a bunch of people at that party, and Devin was already a pile of goo in his bedroom when I found him. There weren't any silver net marks on him, so I don't know why you're showing me a net that's not mine."

My lawyer cleared his throat. "Mr. Jensen, I strongly urge you to—"

"I didn't do *anything*," I said.

"Were you aware the net has blood all over it?" the detective asked.

So this was what it was like talking to a wall. More like bashing my head against it for shits and giggles and probably some jail time. More than some. Shit.

"How could I be aware of the blood if I've never seen the net before?" I asked.

Detective Nuyen lifted an eyebrow as he glanced down at the folder. "Did you know much about Devin's past other than what I've told you?"

I knew enough to want him dead and to never feel sorry about it, especially if it was by my own hand but even if it wasn't. "No."

He flipped to the second page in the folder. "About twenty-five years ago, he schmoozed with the upper levels of the Southern Clan society. Upper, *upper* levels. He was part of the Southern Clan queen's harem, the last of them alive."

The same queen who'd vanished and then later turned up murdered. Bronwen was her name, a real beauty, at least she had been when I happened to catch her on VTV, and ruler over the Southern Clan. After she died, her sister took over, and everything went to shit. So was Bronwen's murder what had triggered Devin to poison himself to become immune to its effects? Because he was afraid someone was going to murder him, too, like the rest of her harem?

I shrugged, completely clueless as to why I was suffering through a history lesson that had little to do with me when there was a strange silver net in my apartment. "I didn't know that. Good for him, I guess."

The detective flipped to the third page. "But it didn't end so good for him, did it?"

That depended on who you asked, I supposed. For Jessica, it was damn good because she'd never have to see the fucker ever again.

A burst of heat shot across my inner wrist, on the other side of where the sun had hit me through the window earlier. What the hell? On top of everything else, was the sun slowly baking through my bones?

A long silence fell over the room, thick and uncomfortable. The only sound was Mr. Phillips's clicking pen, slowing like a dying heartbeat, as he frowned down at the notes he'd taken. Detective Nuyen stood there unmoving while staring at the third page in the white folder.

Finally, he looked up at me and laid the folder on the table with great care. "It's also not looking good for you, Ashe. Not at all."

The solemn note in his voice charged a rush of unease up my spine. "Yeah. I can see that."

"Can you? Because that silver net in your apartment..." He studied me as he began to pace like I might be able to finish his sentence for him.

I tracked his movements, trying to decipher where he was going with this. No fucking clue.

My inner wrist sizzled again, sharp and painful, but I had other things to worry about besides my baking bones.

"The silver net had trace amounts of blood on it." His size devoured the room while he paced, seeming to pull in the walls around me. "So I'll ask again. Do you know whose blood?"

I shook my head. "You'd have to ask whoever planted it there."

"It's Bronwen's, Ashe." Detective Nuyen stopped and stared me down, the implication in his words like the *snick* of a lock. "Former Queen Bronwen's blood is on that net in your apartment. Which means I'll be charging you for her murder as well."

Mr. Phillips began talking a mile a minute, but I couldn't hear anything. I had too many questions, too many impossibilities running through my head, so I just sat there, completely stunned.

Charged for murdering clan royalty and a member of her harem. Two royal murders I didn't commit. That crime carried the harshest punishment—death. Swift if I were lucky. Prolonged torture if the current queen had anything to do with it.

I needed to get the fuck out of here.

CHAPTER FIVE

WREN

"How many guards do you see?" Zac asked, squinting into the darkness like his human eyes could catch something mine couldn't.

"Two. Humans with rifles. Likely more inside and around back." With the buzzing cicadas and relentless chirping crickets, I had to speak at a louder volume than I wanted. If it were only humans out there, it wouldn't be an issue. I, on the other hand, could hear an ant fart if I concentrated hard enough. It was safe to assume other vampires could do the same.

"When are visiting hours?" I asked, but I had a growing suspicion that visiting hours wouldn't matter.

"Who said we're visiting him?"

I smacked my forehead and groaned. "I should have killed you back in Silversage. This is suicide."

"This is perfect," he said. "It will be sunrise soon, the perfect time to break a vampire out of jail since the vampire guards can't follow. We just have to make it to your car and not get separated." He held my gaze. "And we won't."

"Like I said..." I looked to the eastern horizon, already shaded with a ribbon of blue and the faintest hint of orange. "Suicide."

Zac held his cell phone and spoke quietly into the speaker like a doctor taking notation. "This is Detective Zac Palmer, here with Melody..." He looked up at me. "What's your last name?"

"Songsmith. At least that's what it says on my ID."

"So you don't know for sure?"

I shook my head, again feeling like an idiot for not having known something so basic. When you're eight, you tend to believe whatever your mom tells you, so I never thought to question it. Like one Christmas when she happened to find a tiny Christmas tree we decorated with snowflakes cut out of newspapers and a foil fast-food wrapper star. I woke up Christmas night to find a Barbie doll dressed in a pink ballerina tutu and no shoes and some scuffed snow boots. She had smiled brightly and said, *"Look what Vampire Santa left! You've been a very good girl this year."* Later I realized she had probably robbed the thrift store. We'd been sleeping in their basement for a couple weeks.

He spoke into the phone again. "Here with Melody Songsmith at an unnamed facility in Brightwell, Louisiana, approximately half a mile south off the three-eighty-two bypass at mile marker fifteen. Time is 0530 hours, the twelfth of August, 2019. Target, a male vampire, first name Ashe, last name unknown. Two guards visible, unknown number inside the location."

"Who are you reporting to, exactly?"

"That's classified."

"Okay. Whatever." If he knew my real name, he was good at hiding it. I'd let him call me Melody for now. Hell, he might be using an alias, too, for all I knew. We weren't chummy enough for real first names yet.

Mosquitoes buzzed by my ears. They never bite me because I'm not exactly alive and all. But they were homing in on Zac. He smacked his cheek, and with that smack came the scent of his fresh, hot blood.

Shit, it smelled good. I paced far enough away to smell the decaying leaves and sickeningly sweet honeysuckle in the woods around us. Between that and this need to find a vampire I had never met, my cold blood boiled, throwing all my senses into overdrive. I could hear the wet splatter of tobacco juice from one of the guards who stood watch outside the jail. Disgusting.

"Did you have a plan of action in mind, Detective, or are we just going to storm the castle? Because right now, I think I can rip all the doors off their hinges."

"If this is the kind of facility I think it is, we'll need more than your vampire strength." He opened Birdie's passenger door and rummaged through one of his bags, then buckled a duty belt around his waist like Batman. He now had two guns holstered and had removed his blazer. Damn, he looked even more lickable all armed and dangerous.

Sniffing the air, I detected the distinct smell of...

"Silver bullets," he said, smiling.

"Is this a rescue mission or an assassination?"

"Depends on how it goes." At my stop-the-bullshit look, he added, "Rescue is the plan, but we're likely to encounter some hostiles."

The symbol on my arm vibrated, sending pinpricks all along my spine. "Let's get this over with."

"Okay, so first we should take out the two guards there in —"

I didn't wait for him to finish. Whatever this sensation or instinct was, it wouldn't let me linger any longer. Not when Ashe was in there, whoever the hell he was.

The chirps and buzzes of crickets and cicadas became one shrill scream as I zipped along the narrow dirt road through the darkness. I let my senses take over, veering off the path through the brush, where I easily dodged trees and thorns and hurtled over fallen logs and crumbling fence posts that housed half-buried rusty barbed wire. It wasn't much different than hunting my mother's killers. Hell, for all I knew, maybe these people had something to do with it. That thought made what I was about to do even easier.

I moved so fast, it must have sounded like a mini tornado. The first guard spun around just as I collided with him. He made an "oomph" sound as I pinned him against a chain-link fence. Though he held his rifle with an iron grip, I ripped it from his hands and flung it aside. The dim security lights reflected the fear in his lazy eye and a rounded chipmunk cheek full of tobacco. I didn't recognize him, but he reeked of the same stench as Rusty and the other rednecks I'd crossed off my list.

"Terry!" he managed to scream before I plunged my fingers into his neck and tore his throat out.

I flung him to the ground, where he gurgled and flailed on the gravel.

His partner, whom I assumed was Terry, aimed a flashlight at me. I squinted into the light and hissed with my fangs fully emerged. Totally for dramatic purposes. It always freaked humans the fuck out.

"Shit!" Terry dropped the flashlight and pointed his rifle with its red laser sight at me.

I darted straight for him. A soft, hollow pop came from somewhere in the woods as I knocked him to the ground and held on. We skidded along the gravel like I was riding a human skateboard. I raised my hand to rip his throat out, but his eyes rolled back in his head. Foam bubbled up from his mouth like a mini science experiment volcano. A very thin dart stuck out from his neck. If that was poison, it sure was some powerful shit.

Zac emerged, running into the clearing from the dirt road, lowering his gun which looked like a Colt .45 with a fat telescopic sight. "What the hell? I didn't mean like that."

"What is that? A dart gun?"

"Yeah, with tranquilizers that would keep them out for a few hours, and you should have let me use it on both guards. If the rest of them didn't know we're here, they do now."

"You said take out the two guards. They're taken out. Now how do we get in this place?" I slung my hand to remove the bits of flesh from the first guard's neck and touched the chain-link fence. It stung like a hornet, but it wasn't electrified. "Shit. Is that –?"

"Silver plated. I told you this was no ordinary jail."

The more I looked around, the more I saw that he was right. The silver-coated fence surrounded a solid concrete building that had tiny slits of windows near the roof. I suspected the shingles also contained bits of silver, considering how they sparkled. Cautiously, I stuck my hand into a sickly yellow shaft of light from one of the security lamps overhead.

"Don't –" Zac said a moment too late. It was fiery hot, like passing your finger through the flame of a candle.

"UV lights."

"Yeah, I thought so. High-powered, too. Like the sun times five."

I paced like a caged animal along the fence line, careful to avoid direct light. "So how do I get past the silver and sunlamps on crack?"

"What do you feel right now?"

"I...feel..." Closing my eyes, I concentrated on the energy that throbbed in my arm and pressed against my subconscious mind. "He's scared, confused, ashamed?" I turned to Zac with a helpless shrug. "All I know is that I have to help him. Why am I feeling this?"

"I'm not sure, but I can get you in there, if you can take out anyone that gets in our way."

"Deal. But if there are any hostile vampires anywhere in the vicinity, that dart gun is useless."

"I know. That's what you're here for. This is for the humans. We don't need any nosy neighbors or cops complicating things."

More lights flared to life just then from the building's roof. They moved spotlight-style along the ground. I dodged one, got clipped by another on the cheek, and took refuge behind Zac.

He checked his phone, then pointed left. "That way. There's a service entrance."

We ran around the corner of the fence. The gravel road dipped down to a flat area where a few vehicles were parked. We ducked between an old Toyota pickup with a bent chassis and busted taillight and an ugly sun-flower gold van.

Zac eased himself up and quickly peered through the passenger window of the van before squatting back down again. "Good. There are keys in the ignition."

"For?"

"We may need a getaway vehicle if we can't make it back to your car before sunup."

"I would say I wouldn't be caught dead in that thing, but..."

He chuckled then gently touched my cheek where the light had left a blistered streak. "Does it hurt?"

"It's fine." I brushed his hand away. What was I supposed to say? That it hurt like a sumbitch and if he touched me like that again, I might drain him dry? I hadn't had a proper meal for a couple days, and a hangry vampire wasn't someone you wanted to hang out with.

Between the sweeping lights, I peeked over the truck to scan the area. There was a wide gate with a thick lock and chain. A heavy silver-plated steel door opened, and out came another human guard, gun raised.

"You'll leave if you know what's good for you!" the guard hollered. He half hid behind the open door and squinted into the parking lot, nervously searching for whatever had triggered the lights. The lights might be torture for vampires, but did nothing to help the humans' already pitiful night vision.

"Stay down," Zac said as he steadied the dart gun on the hood and pulled the trigger.

The guard fell out of the door and onto the concrete stoop. His body flopped like a dying fish sprawled on the steps. The door swung shut again with a bang that echoed through the night.

"If you're trying to keep this quiet, you're doing a shitty job of it," I said.

A rat—spooked from all the ruckus, no doubt—scampered out from under the truck. I snatched it up and sank my fangs into its jugular, drinking deeply until its pulse faded. Tossing its carcass aside, I wiped my mouth with a napkin I found discarded on the ground next to a crushed cheeseburger wrapper and foam cup.

I looked up to find Zac grimacing at me. "What? I was hungry."

"A rat? I mean...that's..."

"Gross? Would you rather me eat *you*?"

"No, but is that a normal thing for vampires?"

I huffed a laugh. "How the fuck would I know?"

"Is that what you ate when your mother..." He bit down on whatever he was going to say. "Sorry, I shouldn't have asked."

A brief image of a spider web-dusted crypt and a scrawny rat ran a chill down my spine. "No, you shouldn't have. Now shut up and get me in there."

He held my gaze for a moment before I tore mine away. Then he slipped over to the gate and took another tool that looked like a tire pressure gauge from his belt. A second later, a red laser started cutting through the chain. The lights circled back around, so I ducked down, feeling like a helpless little girl again.

I'd never tried to explain my circumstances to anyone before. Now that I had to rehash the shit-fest that was my non-life, it all sounded so pathetic. Maybe I should have been like those bloodthirsty creatures in the movies, killing at will and not giving a fuck. My mother would have been no less dead. I would have been no less alone, and maybe I would have already met a special vampire by now. Especially now that I knew others like me existed.

"Melody!" At Zac's loud whisper, I peeked cautiously over the truck again. The insta-sunburn lights were out. He had gone through the gate and now stood by a silver-plated electrical box. He motioned me over.

I breezed through the gate, careful to avoid the metal.

"I cut the wires," he whispered, grinning like he'd performed some magical feat.

"What do you want? A cookie?"

"No. But I've cut power to most of the building, I think. They wasted a lot of time and money vampire-proofing the place. Guess they didn't think to human-proof it. Shall we kick some ass and find your vampire?"

"I thought you'd never ask." We opened the service door and sneaked inside. I led the way, since the only light came from very dim emergency lights on either side of what looked like a large storage room. Crates and boxes lined the walls. Shelves holding guns and ammo and various silver items – nets, locks, pliers, and a whole host of torturous-looking implements – took up one of the narrower walls.

Fast, heavy footsteps echoed from a stairwell across the room. Narrow points of red light bounced along the walls. I sniffed the air – more human guards. About three of them from the sound of it.

Zac started forward.

I grabbed his arm. "No, I got this."

I zoomed ahead before he could stop me and met the guards halfway up the stairs. The rest of it went down in about five seconds.

Here's the slow-mo version:

Fangs bared, I hissed like an angry cat. Human guard One froze dead in his tracks and pointed his gun at my head. His buddies, Two and Three, were going so fast, they rear-ended him, which knocked him off-balance. The gun went off, blowing out the emergency light above us.

Glass rained down as I tore the gun away from him and drove it through his beer gut. Down went One. I kicked him aside. Two pointed his gun, but his arms shook so bad, the laser sight bounced all over the place. I yanked the gun from One's gut like a redneck version of Excalibur and shot Two with it. Down went Two.

Three hightailed it up the stairs, but I grabbed his leg and dug my fingers in. He shrieked and dropped his gun. It clattered down the steps as I reeled him in and flipped him over. This one would be dinner. I sank my fangs into his neck, ignoring his shrieks as I gulped down his life like he had probably chugged down beer.

Something moved on the stairs below me. I sprang up and pounced. My hands were around Zac's neck before I realized I had pinned him against the wall. His pulse beat like a war drum under my fingers.

"Melody, it's me."

I leaned in close, inhaling his warm, rapid breaths. "Why shouldn't I? Why shouldn't I obey my instincts?"

"Because you need me. Alive."

Boy did he ever feel alive, his skin hot and sweaty beneath my palms. I pressed closer against his firm body until his racing heart thumped a seductive rhythm on my tits.

Withdrawing enough to look into his eyes, I saw fear, mixed with longing and loneliness. It was like looking into a mirror. I wanted his blood so badly I could imagine its hot, metallic thickness flowing across my tongue and down my throat. But then the tattoo on my wrist shot a jolt of electricity up my arm and jarred me back into reality. I swallowed hard. Zac might have been an idiot to get involved with me, but he could be my only chance at bringing down the rest of my mother's killers.

The hunger subsided.

"I'm sorry," I whispered and let him go. "I didn't mean to."

He stood up straight and rubbed his neck, not meeting my gaze. "We don't have time for– Get down!"

I ducked. Zac fired a shot up the stairs. Another body tumbled, writhing and howling like an animal, like something not human. I looked down into yellow eyes, bared fangs, and a hole pouring thick, nearly black blood from his shoulder. He had on a uniform like the other guards, but he wasn't like the other guards.

"You're a vampire," I whispered.

He hissed at me. "No shit, Sher—" and then his eyes went wide. "Bronwen? How the fuck are you alive? You won't be for long when Queen Ravana finds out about this."

Hearing my mother's name lifted all the hairs on the back of my neck. "How do you know my mother? Who's Ravana?"

"*Mother*? Holy shit! Bronwen had a kid?" He shook his head with a wheezy laugh. "Did you come here to kill him?"

Kill him? Kill who?

Another shot startled me. A hole oozed blood and molten silver from the vampire's forehead.

"Come on!" Zac went ahead, stepping over the first vampire I'd ever seen, besides my mother, stopping only to tear the ID from where it was clipped on the vampire's belt loop.

I followed, lost in a cloud of overwhelming confusion. "What did he mean, kill him? Kill who?"

"Ravings of a mad vampire. Did you see his skin? I think he was a meth head."

"Vampires do meth?"

"No, they drink blood from meth heads. Same effect."

We emerged onto the main floor where rows of silver-plated steel doors lined the walls. Jail cells, I guessed. Each door was inset with tiny windows. Shadows flashed by them. I looked at one such window as we passed.

A pair of yellow eyes appeared suddenly, which scared the shit out of me, even though I knew very well that these were my "people," if you could call them that. As we crept along the hallway, more eyes followed us from every window. Pleas and shocked cries echoed from within the cells.

"It's her! It's Bronwen."

"My queen! Get me out of here, would ya'?"

"She gonna fuck Ravana up!"

We were coming up on another corridor that crossed the one we were in. That could pose a big risk for ambush. But my distracted mind was still trying to make some sense of the nonsensical. Apparently they thought I was my mother and a queen. Maybe they were all druggies, but I'd heard another name twice.

"Who's Ravana?" I whispered to Zac.

He held a finger to his lips and blocked my way with his other arm. "We have company."

From the left came a blur of movement. Zac couldn't get a shot off in time. A vampire guard tackled him, throwing him to the floor. Zac's head banged against the concrete.

I grabbed the vampire's collar and belt before he could deliver a lethal bite and threw him against a cell door with a clang that echoed through the building and vibrated the floor. He shrieked as his arm made contact with the silver door. I glanced at Zac, who appeared to be out cold, hopefully not dead.

The vampire rolled to a crouch and sprang at me then knocked me to my back. But I didn't give him a chance to pin my arms and legs. I kicked and threw him over my head, directly into another guard who had just emerged from the other corridor.

Flipping to all fours, I stayed between them and Zac, who was slowly coming around, and gave them a full-fanged hiss. It wasn't an act like before. This hiss came from somewhere deep and dark and instinctual.

They started forward again but suddenly froze, their yellow eyes widening, glowing with a mix of shock and fear.

One of them got control of his senses enough to whisper, "It's... No, it can't be. Queen Bronwen? Is it really you?"

Two shots rang out. They fell limp to the floor, silver bubbling from the holes in their chests. They melted into gooey globs of flesh a second later. I turned to see Zac sitting up, gun still aimed as though they might spring back to unlife any second.

I jumped to my feet. "Why did you kill them? We could have gotten information from them."

"Trust me. You don't want them alive. They're not on your side." He slowly got to his feet, wincing as he rubbed the back of his head.

"What are you not telling me? I swear I will rip your balls off and make you choke on 'em if you're hiding some—" But before I could carry out immediate castration, my symbol lit up like a Christmas tree. Energy zinged up my arm, pulling me forward to the last door on the right of the main corridor.

Zac followed. I peered into the window, careful not to touch the door. I could see nothing but total darkness. No sounds from within either.

"You think he's in there?" Zac asked.

"I don't know for sure. Can you open it?"

"Let's see if this works." Zac touched the first vampire guard's ID on a red laser scanner by the cell door. It slid open leisurely like we were about to step into a Walmart.

The dim emergency lights did little to illuminate the pitch darkness. My night vision revealed a cot with a crumpled blanket and pillow, a bloody cloth and a cool blue shape hunched in the far corner. Almost like...a man?

"Ashe?" I whispered.

A head lifted, and copper-colored eyes locked on mine.

"Is that your name? Are you Ashe?"

He answered with a full-fanged snarl and hurled himself at us. I zipped in to block him, punching him in the chest with the heel of my hand. He flew back onto the cot, legs flying over his head, and toppled off the other side.

A tiny groan followed. "Ow."

I ran inside, now afraid I'd killed this vampire I didn't know but *had* to find. The two symbols on my arm stopped buzzing and instead turned to a steady warm sensation that flowed over my cold skin like a towel fresh from the dryer.

I spent a millisecond too long basking in that warmth. When I looked back up, he was right beside me. In a blur, he picked me up and threw me down onto the cot. The springs under the terrible mattress screeched at the injustice. I saw movement from the corner of my eye. Zac pointed his gun right at Ashe's head.

"No! Don't!" I looked back up into the face of this stranger with beautiful copper eyes, full lips, and short sandy-brown hair. He wasn't hurting me, just staring at my face as though he'd never seen anything like me before.

My mind struggled to find something not stupid to say. I mean, what the fuck do you say to a vampire you've just sprung from jail? A vampire who might kill you or fuck you, and more disturbingly, knowing you'd let him do either without a fight?

CHAPTER SIX

ASHE

UH, WHAT THE FUCK just happened? One minute, I was lying on my lumpy bed in my cell, listening to the fading sounds of some huge fight somewhere in the jail, and the next, I was getting punched in the chest by the most stunningly beautiful woman I'd ever seen. And she looked familiar, like Queen Bronwen. But Queen Bronwen was dead, and I was here in part because the police thought I killed her with a silver net. So this couldn't be Bronwen.

But as soon as I saw her, the painful, sizzling heat on my wrist morphed into a warm tingle that took over my entire body like a steady hum. Need, sharper than any thirst I'd ever felt, coursed through me, as well as a powerful urge to protect her.

I threw her on the bed because I...well, I needed to see her underneath me. My dick made me do strange things sometimes, especially right now, pressed against her inner thigh, harder than I'd ever been. She stared up at me through the messy bangs of her short, very blonde hair, her eyes a pale green even though she moved like a vampire. Contacts, I guessed later, because right then I was thinking about wild monkey sex.

Heat grew between her legs as she shifted, her body fitting to mine perfectly. My hips twitched forward on their own to feel her soft curves wrap around me a little tighter, and her full lips parted. A vixen-like grin spread across her mouth as she brought her hand to my ass and squeezed.

"How about you let me finish rescuing you before we get to that, inmate," she said, her voice like whiskey and smoke.

Someone cleared their throat behind us. "Best idea I've heard yet," an irritated male voice said.

As if I'd been dunked headfirst into a holy-water-filled bathtub, I tore myself off of her and stumbled into the opposite wall of my cell. Sweet Vampire Jesus, that whole encounter on the cot must've only lasted about five seconds, but I'd been humping the hot girl while some guy—a DBD from the smell of him—with dark hair, red eyes that appeared to be contacts, a chin dimple, and a big-ass gun looked on, *while I was still in jail*. Not my best day ever.

Loud voices sounded from down the hall. The three of us stared at each other in the panicked split-second it took before we sprang into action. I dove for the bed, volunteering myself to hide the woman with my whole body. But she rolled from the mattress and slid underneath the bed in a way that made me think she did this kind of thing every day. The guy was already closing the door of my cell and then folded himself into the corner.

Quick footsteps echoed closer. For someone who'd been accused of two murders, who'd actually planned a murder from beginning to end, funny that I didn't know if I could stomach witnessing a bloody one in the confines of my cell.

More shouts. More footsteps. Even closer.

As long as I protected the woman underneath my bed, I would do what I had to do though.

Metal clanged as the footsteps came closer. It sounded like they were beating on the cell doors and likely peering inside the glass windows at the top. If they did, we were screwed. I wrenched the scratchy blanket out from under me and threw part of it over the edge of the bed to cover the woman.

Bang. Bang. Pause. "What the fuck?"

My jail cell exploded with action, a thousand moving parts at once. The door burst open. A flood of guards poured in, guns drawn and loaded with silver-tipped bullets. The chin-dimple guy in the corner rounded on them, a distraction that would last only seconds.

I lunged off the bed to stand in front of it, but the woman had already shot out from underneath it. Her pale green eyes narrowed into lethal slits as she flashed toward the guards. Shots rang out. Bullets zinged between the metal walls, sparking as they made contact. My confused-as-hell body screamed at me to simultaneously run, to drop to the ground, to stand perfectly still. We had to get out of this deathtrap.

But the woman... She kicked and punched with expert skill, each strike perfectly placed and timed. Enough to incapacitate before she delivered the final blow—a broken neck. Bodies piled up around her, most from her doing, but the guy swung the butt of his big-ass gun to drop several too.

Until no one was left standing except them. And me, staring like a jackass with my mouth hanging to my shins.

"Who are you?" I asked.

The woman turned and grinned. "Your new best friends. Ready to get out of here?"

There was no way I could say no. If they wanted me dead, they wouldn't be offering to bust me out. At least, I hoped.

"Melody. Ashe," the chin-dimple guy behind her said gruffly, kneeling by one of the dropped guards. "Get a guard's uniform on. It'll help us get out of here faster."

"And put this on," the woman—Melody—said and threw something furry and alive at me.

I caught it. A cat? Nope. And not alive either. It was a curly brown wig. "Good plan."

"I thought so." Nodding, she began unbuttoning a guard's bloodied shirt.

They knew my name. Knew I was in trouble and needed to get out. "Why me?" I asked them. "Why are you here for me?"

Melody stood with the guard's shirt and shrugged into it, hiding all of her plentiful curves tucked inside her black tank top and black pants. She had a rose vine tattoo that climbed all the way up one shoulder and another tattoo on her wrist. A circle with a single diamond shape stretching from the center outward. Just like mine. Well, that was weird. That must have been where the tingling had come from, and the tattoo had just...appeared.

Her mouth opened and shut a few times as her agile fingers worked the shirt buttons shut, as if maybe she wasn't quite sure what she was doing here. "We're here for you because you have answers?"

"I have *questions*."

Chin Dimple threw me a shirt and pants with a no-nonsense, I-will-stake-you-with-a-toothpick look. "You have one second to put those on."

The blood donor had balls, I'd give him that. He'd waltzed into a vampire jail as tonight's buffet and didn't seem to give a fuck. But again, why? And why for me?

Melody threw him a wig with longer dark hair than he already had. Then she put on a sandy brown one over her platinum hair. She looked like she'd blend in with her disguise, but she was still just as gorgeous as before.

I dressed quickly and wigged myself, seeing that the other two were already done, then bent to retrieve one of the fallen weapons.

"You ever shot one of those before?" Dimple asked, peering out the cell door.

The gun felt heavy and strange in my hands. "Never."

"Just don't shoot me or Melody, and you'll be good." Another glance down the hallway, and then, "Let's go."

The three of us strode out the open door. The other two flanked me as if I were as valuable as gold or something. The other inmates had their faces pressed to the windows in their doors to see what was going on.

"What's happening out there?" one demanded.

"Hey, talk to us, assholes," another shouted.

The three of us kept our gazes stuck to the floor. As soon as we could, we swung left down a different hallway, leaving the other inmates behind. We walked at a steady clip, but I itched to run as fast as I could.

"Ashe." Melody's wrist bumped into mine, and a wild energy crashed through my skin at the contact. "If we see someone coming, you can't look like that."

"Like what?"

She grinned. "Like you're about to taste freedom. Look pissed or something."

Out of nowhere, Dimple's gun smacked me in the back of the head. "There," he growled. "Now he looks pissed."

"The fuck?" Before I could throat punch him, the doors at the end of the hallway banged open.

Vampire guards poured through. One of them eyed us and then pointed in the direction he was heading.

"With me," he barked. "Now."

He swept next to Dimple, grabbed his sleeve, and shoved him in the direction he wanted him to go. Dimple looked back and met our gazes, his "oh" expression connecting with Melody's hissed "shit."

The guy grabbed the back of Dimple's neck and shoved him again. "Move it! Security breach 0204. One man, one woman. Let's act like we care."

The other guards moved in behind them, but the rough guy was starting to look back in our direction, likely to yell at us to join in the fun too. Melody was already taking my hand and steering us through a stairway door, just in time.

"It's okay. He knows the plan. He'll be there." Melody's grip tightened in mine as we descended the stairs.

"Be where?"

"In a getaway van outside."

I glanced at the shaded windows as we passed them, at the soft light slipping underneath the cracks. It would be daylight soon, the perfect time for a break from vampire jail since vampires couldn't run out into the sun to give chase. But not so perfect if you didn't have a getaway driver.

"As in a getaway van outside *in the sun*?" I asked.

"Yep."

"And where will we be?"

"Waiting for him to come to pick us up."

I guessed that the van wasn't parked at the curb, then. Too obvious. Too suspicious. "And if he doesn't?"

She didn't answer. She didn't have to.

One of us was going to have to go outside and get the van. And I'd be damned if I let it be her.

So I did what I always did in these types of situations. Well, not this situation exactly since this was my first jail break, but I blended into the role of desperate, innocent vampire who needed *out*. Not terribly hard, and for the details I needed to do that, I would fake it until I made it.

"Where's the van?" I asked.

"It's the first ugly gold one in the southeast lot. Looks like some kind of 1970s rape van. Can't miss it. Keys are in the ignition, but you can't be thinking—"

A door below us slammed open, and Melody immediately released my hand. A guard ran up the stairs and right past us as if his ass were on fire.

As soon as he was out of earshot, I said, "We need to get to the roof."

She stared hard at me as we rounded the landing onto another set of stairs. "You *are* thinking about going out there. No. No way. We need to get to security and see if we can find Zac on the working cameras. We're not leaving here without him."

"He's important to you?" Yeah, bad timing, but there it was.

"Well..." She took my hand again and squeezed. "He got me in here to rescue you."

"So *I'm* important?"

"You have to feel it." She moved our clasped hands in front of us and pointed at our wrists. "Right here."

"Yeah, I feel it." There, and other places. "Where's security?"

"First floor."

"And they'll just let us in to have a peek at their cameras, will they?"

She grinned, one that made my whole body react. "I don't see why not."

On the first floor, we found the door marked Security. The hallway was empty except for a vampire in silver cuffs around his ankles and two guards quickly escorting him into a room.

I tried the door. "Locked," I muttered.

She held out a ring of keys and twirled them around her finger. "I wonder if these will come in handy."

I snatched them from her, unable to keep the smile from my face. She was having entirely too much fun. Once the door was unlocked, we slid in one body part at a time in case we weren't alone. Voices sounded from an adjoining room behind a closed door. We needed to be silent and quick.

Melody scanned the monitors along the wall while I searched the desk drawers. If I was going to be the getaway driver, I needed distractions to keep the focus off of me. The more the better. I found a lighter, a mostly empty glass bottle of Jack Daniels, and someone's smelly sock. That would do. I also found a map of the jail and how to access the roof.

"There he is," Melody muttered, pointing at one of the screens. "Third floo-- What the hell?"

I turned in time to see Chin Dimple fling something at the feet of the vampire guards surrounding him and then take off running. It exploded into a flash of violent monochrome light, followed by a dense cloud of thick black ashes. A UV bomb? Damn.

Quickly, I took Melody's hand and led her out of the security room, my skin buzzing at the contact. "Go. Intercept him. Then get to the front door."

She looked at me with big yellow eyes. She must've taken out her green contacts to better blend in, and I couldn't decide which I liked better, a detail that didn't matter right now.

"You'll be there?" she asked. "At the front door too?"

"I'll be there."

She looked behind her at the empty hallway and then back at me with a wicked smile. "Look at the balls on you."

I winked. "They're not nearly as impressive as the rest of me."

Grinning, she stepped away from me, her fingertips hooking around mine. "Go. Fast. Or I'll have to come rescue you again."

I nodded. "Let's try not to make that a habit."

I turned and left her behind, hating every inch of myself for doing so. This was insanity, fueled by an intoxicating promise of freedom. The sun would be up soon, and I was about to hurl myself out into it for a little daytime, rooftop picnic. Even worse, Melody depended on me not to fail. So I couldn't. Yeah, I'd just met her, but still. She'd risked her life to break me out for no reason I could guess other than this weird connection. But it felt right. *She* felt right.

I stuck to the stairs, acting like I had every right to be there in my guard's uniform. Groups of them flew past me without a glance as they shouted orders back and forth, totally oblivious to Inmate 204 running by.

On the top floor, a ladder stretched up the wall to the rooftop, and once I opened the door that led out, the orange streak in the sky slammed into me like a wall, bouncing me back inside. That would've been the smart thing to do. Instead, my legs weighted to the max with doubt, I stepped outside.

I had just minutes, tops, before sunrise.

In the distance, a helicopter whirred, not visible yet, but I had a feeling that was about to change.

I sprinted for the southeast corner of the building, pouring on my vampire speed and whatever other kinds of speeds I happened to have. Before the edge, I slowed, spotted an open dumpster below to my right, and jumped. *Damn*. And shot out of that stink like I'd just sat on a blowtorch. But not before setting the inside of the dumpster on fire with a splash of Jack from the bottle and the lighter I'd taken.

Then I spotted the gold van about fifteen yards away, past a dead lawn and the fenced-in work shed. Ugly was right. Not at all inconspicuous, but beggars can't be choosers. I ran toward it, my skin prickling with heat.

The orange streak in the sky had grown, now with bright yellow smudges. I gritted my teeth against my growing panic. No more looking at the sky. Ever.

When my feet hit the parking lot, the helicopter whirred closer, sounding almost right on top of me. I dropped and scooted underneath the van. The helicopter's shadow crawled over the cement, a huge bug with rotating legs. I bet it was vampire proof.

Frustration burned into my hands until they clenched into fists. I didn't have time for helicopters. The fact that I saw its shadow on the ground wasn't a good sign. Eventually, after I bit down so hard on my teeth that I thought my eardrums had cracked, the whirring faded.

Time to move.

But first, a little fire. I fished out the glass bottle stuffed with the sock and lighter from my pockets, soaked the sock with the rest of the Jack Daniels, wedged it inside the bottle, and struck a flame to the cloth. Then I rolled the bottle across the ground as hard as I could. My troubled youth had taught me it wouldn't actually explode any cars, but it would sure cause the pressurized struts and shock absorbers to fly around like bullets. Another distraction. Which was exactly what we needed.

I hauled ass out from underneath the van. Blinding light pummeled down on top of me. No time to think about it. I tried the driver's side door of the gold van. Locked. Tried again. Still locked or stuck *or holy fucking shit*.

"You're kidding me," I hissed.

Heat ripped down my back. A faint sizzling started up my skin, growing louder.

Through the window, the keys were in the ignition. Locked inside the van. Smoke wafted up from underneath my collar, the tips of my ears, my whole body a match about to be lit.

I gripped the handle and tore the door clean off. A short-term solution since I still had to drive the damn thing. I threw myself inside, cranked the engine, and peeled out of there.

In the rearview mirror, the flames started from my sock cocktail caught on a tire of another car. Somewhere in the distance, over the roar of the engine, the helicopter whirred again.

Smoke still lifted off my body, though less now since the van had a tinted windshield. My hands were blistered and red, and my whole body felt like I'd thrown myself into an oven, but I was still alive.

I squealed to a stop in front of the jail. No sign of Melody or the other guy. I couldn't wait for them. No, fuck that, I *had* to wait for them because they'd risked everything to break me out, a stranger neither of them knew. For all they knew, I *was* a killer. Who would do something like that for me? And what was with this crazy connection I felt to Melody?

So where was she? I was a sitting duck. A stupid sitting duck in a doorless van that would pour in sunlight as soon as I cleared the building.

The helicopter drew closer, but I didn't dare peel my eyeballs away from the front door to look for it.

My wrist burned, rivalling the heat of the sun, and then she burst through the doors. Chin Dimple ran on her heels, and seconds later, a whole slew of pissed-off guards, guns drawn, but they weren't brave enough to fling themselves out into the sun.

Brave. Stupid. It was all a matter of perception.

Bullets flew.

I dived out of the seat into the back so Melody and Dimple could fly in after me. Smoke wafted around Melody. Her face reddened. The sizzling started up and then intensified, and she still had about ten feet to go.

Guns kept firing.

"Run zigzag so you don't get hit!" I shouted, but I could barely hear myself.

And then they were tumbling in, first Melody, then Dimple. The van shot forward with Dimple at the wheel, knocking Melody into me until we lay flat in the back. I held her close, the searing in my wrist fading into calm warmth.

"Are you all right?" she asked, her hand over my dead heart, staring down at me with big, beautiful yellow eyes.

She was asking me that. *Me*. Even while her own skin was smoking and blistering.

I laughed as bullets hit the back of the van, and we got the hell out of there. She laughed, too, as she melted into me with relief. Her body against mine caused all sorts of dirty thoughts to run through my head, even after a jailbreak. Especially after a jailbreak. But I was also aware that we'd both just stepped out into the sun and needed time to heal. Time to run.

Her chin trembled as her gorgeous eyes met mine again. "My real name is Wren."

"It could be Bertha for all I care. Thank you." I was free, all because of Wren and that other guy.

Whoever this Wren woman was, she was gorgeous and deadly, like silver poison in an unbreakable vial. And I desperately wanted a taste.

CHAPTER SEVEN

WREN

"ARE YOU TWO OKAY back there?" Zac yelled over his shoulder. He drove like a maniac on a tiny gravel road not meant for anything with wheels.

"If you can call okay feeling like I'm in a rock tumbler, sure." I held on to the only semi-steady thing in the van —Ashe, who had wedged himself against the back corner and the wheel well.

It didn't have the cushy upholstery of a minivan, just an empty cargo space. But it lacked any windows except those in the front. Depending on which way Zac turned the van, sunlight randomly invaded the interior through a couple of bullet holes in the windshield and the rear doors. Every time it shone through, it managed to hit skin that had already been burned. The tops of my ears were blistered, as were my hands. I could tell my face had sustained a mega sunburn as well, though I couldn't bring myself to touch it.

Smoke still rose from poor Ashe's back. His hands had blisters that were already clearing up before my eyes. He could heal quicker than I could, apparently.

Ashe sat up a bit and took off his stolen guard's shirt. Pity he still had his original one on under it, but at least it got me a few millimeters closer to his skin. Then he grabbed a folded up windshield sunshade that stuck out from under a black garbage bag full of stuffed animals of all things. I grabbed a purple duck that had fallen out during our wild ride and snuggled it beneath my chin as I nestled closer into Ashe's embrace.

With a soft smile, he unfolded the sunshade and draped it over us. "That should keep the sun off you, until we get to wherever we're going. So...where are we going?"

I ventured a look up into Ashe's copper eyes, which were filled with worry and wonder and something deeper that sent fire to my core. It was a much more pleasant feeling than the fire crawling across my skin as it struggled to heal itself.

"I'm not sure," I admitted.

"You look so much like—"

"My mother?"

"Bronwen was your mom?" He swallowed hard and averted his eyes, as though seeing her in me struck a bad nerve.

"Yeah. Did you know her?"

He shook his head. "I saw her a few times on VTV. That's all."

"VTV?"

Zac made another sharp turn, jarring us against the wall of the van.

"Hey! Take it easy!" Ashe held me tighter, which squeezed my ribs like a hungry boa constrictor, but hey, I wasn't about to complain. I was concentrating on how well his hard angles fit against my curves. And his scent – it was intoxicating, like fresh cut cedar.

"I know what I'm doing, thanks," Zac yelled back. Now that we'd rescued Ashe, which I'd have to remind Zac was *his* idea, he was acting like a dick about it. Almost as though he was jealous.

I sat up and peered out the windshield. He was taking us deep into a wooded area. The thick canopy blocked the sunlight, thankfully. Was that why he was taking us farther into the boonies?

"Don't worry about the sun," I said to Zac. "We can stay covered up well enough."

"I'm not worried about the sun. More worried about the chopper. I think I can lose them in here. We'll be able to circle back into town so we can ditch the van in a parking garage. You two can hide in here while I go rent another one."

"What about Birdie?" I asked. "We can't just leave her there. My whole damn life is in that car."

"We'll get you somewhere safe, then I'll make sure you get your car back safe and sound."

"I hope you know where you're going," Ashe said.

"GPS is my friend."

I laughed. "If you get us lost in a nest of horny inbred rednecks, I'll offer you up first."

He narrowed his eyes at me in the rearview mirror.

Now that we weren't being shaken until our fangs rattled, Ashe helped me sit up with my back against the wheel well, facing him. "You're not healing very quickly, Wren. When's the last time you ate?"

I sneaked a peek at the rearview mirror, where amusement flashed in Zac's eyes. "Well, I snacked on a guard at the prison and before that...um, a rat."

"A rat? Are you on some kind of weight-loss diet? You don't need to be, trust me."

"Um, thanks, I guess. But no, that's just what I eat sometimes."

"Whatever floats your boat. What kind of DBDs do you like? I know a good place with great-tasting ABs and a few Os, but they're kind of expensive."

I blinked at him, realizing I must seem like a total idiot for not knowing all those acronyms. Maybe I'd heard them before and had forgotten? Maybe the sun had melted my brain so part of it had leaked from my ears. There were so many questions swirling in my head, I didn't know where to start.

"You don't know what DBDs are, do you?" Ashe asked.

I shook my head.

He gently bit his thumb, lifted my hand, and streaked his blood across the blistered skin. It bubbled and soaked in. The blisters shrank and disappeared, leaving my skin smooth again.

Staring at it, I recalled a day when I was maybe five or six. My mother and I were staying at a motel somewhere in Texas and had just watched *Interview with the Vampire* the night before on TV. The scene where Brad Pitt as Louis watches the sun rise for the last time as a human really stuck with me. I probably didn't understand that he wasn't a vampire, and he looked so warm and handsome in the golden glow of morning.

We had gone to bed before sunup as usual, the heavy drapes pulled across the window to keep out the daylight as we slept. I woke up and saw the light peeking from the edges of the curtains, thinking that maybe I could see the sunrise just like Louis did. So I crept out of bed and crawled under the curtain. I did indeed see the beautiful orange and pink glow of sunrise as it silhouetted the *Adult XXX Emporium* sign across the road. For about two seconds, I was mesmerized, until the sun popped fully over the sign. My face immediately heated to what felt like two thousand degrees.

I screamed. My mother was there in a flash. She grabbed me and bounded into the space between the two double beds. I was crying so hard, I didn't understand what she was doing, but now I remembered her biting her thumb and rubbing it over my skin. I had always assumed she was just drying my tears. But the burn subsided quickly. That's when she told me the only sunrises we could see were on TV, that being in the sun for longer than a few seconds could be deadly to us. I'd managed to avoid the sun fairly well since then...until today.

Ashe repeated the process on my other hand and was applying his blood to my forehead when I snapped back into reality. His blood smelled like him times five, with the distinct twang of old, dead blood like I'd smelled in Hotel Enigma. I took his hand and flipped his wrist over, then brought it to my lips.

I felt him tense up, like he might yank his hand away, but instead, he watched me with a steely intensity as I gently bit down and sucked up some of his cold, thick blood. It tasted even better than it smelled, not like food really, but more like a blood-flavored medicine. The effects were immediate. I could feel my skin tingle and stretch as the remaining blisters faded away.

I sucked again, swallowed more. All my senses fired at once. My eyes read Ashe's cool blue temperature signature, along with the reddish purple of a slightly warmer area in his crotch. My ears picked up on the *tha-thump, tha-thump* of Zac's heart.

"Wren, that's enough." Ashe slowly pulled his wrist away.

I jerked it back to my mouth, bit down, and sucked. I needed more. Lots more.

"I said, that's enough!" He withdrew forcefully that time, darting to the other side of the van. He wrapped the fingers of his other hand tight around his wrist, staring at me as though he was caged with a starving lion.

"What's going on back there?" Zac asked. "Wren, you okay?"

Wren, not Melody. He must've overheard me when I told Ashe.

I drew my knees to my chest and covered my face. "I'm sorry. I don't know what the shit came over me."

"It's fine. We're all fine," Ashe said. "Wren's just tired and needs a decent meal. I suggest we find a suitable place for her to eat so she won't have to chew off that chin dimple of yours. Uh, what's your name anyway?"

I'd failed to introduce the two of them, my human guide and vampire insta-boyfriend. A minor infraction compared to me trying to feast on Ashe and my cluelessness about my own kind.

"Palmer. Zac Palmer."

Was it just my imagination, or had Zac lowered his voice and applied a British accent?

Ashe must have noticed, too, considering the way he imitated Zac. "A real life James Bond in our midst, eh? Must be our bloody fucking jolly good luck. How's about a spot of tea, govna?"

I lifted my head. "That was a terrible impression."

"Hey, he started it," Ashe said, tilting his head toward Zac. "But at least you're smiling now."

He was right. I was smiling. For a moment, it felt oddly comfortable here in the midst of these two guys who I didn't even know forty-eight hours ago. The feeling was even stronger with Ashe, like I'd known him my whole life, even though I didn't know him from Vampire Adam.

Zac consulted his phone screen again. "Stay down. I'm pulling out onto the bypass. The sun might be a little bright."

Ashe gestured me back to him, so I scooted up close. He turned me so I sat with my back facing him, right up against his chest between his legs. He held the sunshade over us like a tent. There didn't seem to be any hesitation on his part, even though I'd attempted to juice him like a lime a minute ago.

Fatigue and the comforting closeness of his body made my eyelids heavy. I sank back onto his shoulder. He turned his face so he supported my lolling head. His cheek rested against my forehead.

I closed my eyes, felt his lips part, felt their soft coolness press against my skin. His hardening dick pressed into my lower back. Desire throbbed where my legs converged. I thought I had to be dreaming. I'd never felt this level of need for anyone before.

"What is this?" I asked groggily, tilting my head to allow his lips to settle onto my temple.

"This what?" he whispered.

"This thing between us?"

His gentle kisses migrated to the top of my ear, their gentle suction drawing a quiet groan from me.

"I don't know for sure." His whisper caressed my face. I let my head fall farther to the side so his lips could play along my neck. "But if my suspicions are right, we won't be alone for long."

I didn't understand what he meant, but I didn't really give a fuck, with his lips resting at the corner of my mouth.

"All I know is," he said, "if I don't kiss you right now, I might go insane."

You know those parts in movies where the hero and heroine are about to share their first kiss? The parts where your eyes go wide and you're sitting on the edge of a saggy motel bed ready to cheer because they're *finally* getting together?

Yeah, well, that didn't happen here.

What happened was Zac slammed on the brakes and screamed, "Mother fucking alligators!"

Our bodies smashed against the wheel well. Ashe's head klunked into mine like two coconuts colliding.

"Sorry!" Zac called over his shoulder. "I didn't hit it. Probably should have."

I peeked at the rearview mirror. He was looking right at me, but quickly averted his eyes and put the van in reverse, which jerked our bodies in the other direction.

"Hey! We may be undead, but we're still alive back here," Ashe said, wincing as he sat up and rubbed his head.

"Huh?"

"You know what I mean. Any sign of the helicopter?"

"It turned east. We're heading west, so we should be able to avoid it."

Ashe sniffed the air. "I smell barbeque and cigars. Where are we?"

"We're about five miles from Rent-a-Van."

"If you see a little shack off the road called Edna's Itchen, can we stop there first?" Ashe asked.

"Itching? That sounds contagious." I ran my fingers through my hair and scooted back to the other side of the van.

The cool feel from his lips still lingered on my face. If I didn't keep my distance, I wasn't sure what I might do. I wanted to bite him and fuck him at the same time. Was this normal vampire attraction? If so, it's probably a good thing that I hadn't encountered any others until now.

Ashe's shoulders sank a bit as his eyes followed me with a longing look. He shook his head and scrubbed a hand over his face. "It used to be Edna's Kitchen, but the K got swept away in a tornado about ten years ago. She never bothered putting it back, so Edna's Itchen it is. She hated the locals calling it that at first, but it stuck like any good nickname and actually helped draw in customers."

"I really don't feel like eating a greasy piece of fried chicken," I said with a grimace.

"You're in luck. She has something just perfect for you." He grinned and slipped into his bad British accent. "Palmer, Zac Palmer can have the greasy chicken."

Zac chuckled. "I like mine extra greasy. I see it up ahead. Where can we park? There's really no shade there in the parking lot."

"Drive around back. Special parking."

I crouched and crept behind the front passenger seat, peeking out carefully in case the sun decided to reflect off a bad chrome bumper. Zac pulled off the road, where sure enough, a wood-sided building sat with a sagging roof and white block letters above the door that read *Edna's itchen*. The front parking lot was full of cars and over-compensating dually pickups. He drove around on a narrow, paved drive to the back of the restaurant. There was a temporary storage facility with several units. Zac pulled up to a drive-up keypad on a white painted steel post.

Ashe joined me, crouching behind the passenger seat. "Key in this code – 80085."

"Okay." Zac sounded skeptical. "Wait a minute, doesn't that spell boobs on a calculator?"

"Yeah, so?" Ashe grinned at me.

Zac rolled his eyes. His right hand rested on his holstered gun while he typed the code in with his left. I sincerely hoped Ashe wasn't leading us into some vampire ambush, where the main course would be Zac. I didn't have the strength to protect him.

The overhead door lifted, and inside lay an empty storage space.

"Drive on in," Ashe said.

"If this is a trap, I'm killing you first."

"Why would I want to kill strangers who sprung me from jail? Talk about biting the hand that feeds you." Ashe glanced at me and chuckled.

"Yeah, yeah, very funny," I said.

Zac drove the van into the storage unit. As soon as the rear bumper cleared, the door lowered, effectively plunging the once bright interior into darkness. Zac killed the engine but left the key on so he had the advantage of the parking lights.

Gun drawn, he slowly got out of the van, prepared for an ambush. Ashe didn't seem to have any reservations about the situation. He sprang to the back of the van, opened the double doors, and hopped out, turning to offer his hand to help me down.

I took it gladly. My head was swimming from hunger, fatigue, and probably a concussion from Zac's reckless driving. When my feet hit the concrete floor, I wobbled. Ashe steadied me with his strong hands and body. If I hadn't been ready to chew my own arm off from hunger, I'd have asked Zac to give us a couple minutes in the back of the van. Not exactly romantic, and I had no idea why I felt this way, except that I knew Ashe wanted it as much as I did.

With this level of horniness, I could only assume that vampire life involved prison breaks, bloodletting, and orgies twenty-four seven.

"So, what now?" Zac asked, circling the van like a caged beast. He slid a narrow-eyed warning glare at Ashe as he passed us.

"You just leave that to me," Ashe said.

Holding my hand, he led me to the rear corner of the storage unit and typed a number into another keypad beside a door with a wire glass window. The lock disengaged. Ashe opened the door, and we entered a stairwell illuminated with dim fluorescent lights.

I hesitated. The last time I'd seen a stairway like this, I'd had to fight off a herd of vampires.

Ashe drew me close and stroked my cheek. "It's okay, I promise."

The aroma of smoky barbeque wafted up the stairwell. "Tell me they're not barbequing vampires down there."

"You like yours rare or well done?"

My eyes went wide.

He laughed and squeezed my hand. "I'm kidding. Come on. Zac can come, too, if that makes you feel better, but he probably won't find the menu to his liking."

AT THE BOTTOM OF the stairs was a small wood-paneled hallway. A coat rack stood right at the bottom that held miscellaneous ball caps, a white apron streaked with dried blood, and a crooked umbrella. Open Sysco boxes sat on the worn linoleum floor, one of which was half full of disposable plastic cups like you'd find in any bathroom. Another held napkins.

We walked down the hallway past stainless steel shelves containing peanut oil, lard, and industrial-sized cans of green beans. Below that were bottles of rubbing alcohol, boxes of sterile gauze, and large bottles of raspberry-flavored liquid iron supplements.

It looked like a typical basement storage area of any ratty diner except for the medical supplies and iron supplements. Surely they didn't add that to the food, or maybe they did. I was quickly discovering how little I knew about both the human and vampire world. My mother had sheltered me to protect me, but in the process had not told me much about our kind or humankind, and after her death, my sole focus had been revenge and surviving long enough to make that happen.

Ashe strode confidently through the place, holding my hand. Zac followed so close behind me, I could feel his warmth radiating on my back. He still held his gun in front of him with both hands, pointing it at the floor.

My mind reeled. How much could I really trust either of them? A sinking feeling chilled my already cold blood as Ashe led us through a set of swinging doors. What if they already knew each other and had teamed up to capture me?

Stupid, thy name is Wren. They had made sure I would be too hungry and exhausted to fight back. I was completely trapped. Nowhere to run, because I had no idea how to get out except for the way we came. Even weakened, though, my speed would far surpass Zac's. I just had to knock him down, take out Ashe, and get out of the line of fire and back up the stairs...

"Well, if it ain't Ashe Jensen!"

A woman's loud voice snapped me out of forming my escape plan. I blinked and realized we had entered what looked like a dingy basement diner, with battery-powered lamps and black tablecloths on a dozen or so round tables. The woman standing in front of us was plump with a head of gray hair pulled back into a bun. She wore a flowered dress and a red, ruffled apron.

She could have easily masqueraded as Mrs. Claus, except she didn't hold a plate of cookies for Santa. Instead she wore blue latex gloves and carried a tray, on which lay a bloody scalpel and a couple of bloody gauze pads.

The smell of blood hit me hard, and my fangs emerged, though I tried to keep my mouth closed to hide them.

"Where you been, darlin'? Haven't seen you in ages. And who's this pretty little thing?" She smiled at me and then peered behind me at Zac, who had just holstered his gun. "We don't allow weapons in here."

"It's okay, Edna," Ashe said. "They're with me. This is Wren, and the human is Zac."

"You a DBD, Zac? I'll have to see your paperwork."

"No, just a regular human. Wren's bodyguard."

With one eyebrow arched, I slid him a look. He shrugged.

"Well, we got plenty of human food upstairs." She focused on me again. "You look really familiar, though I can't place the name."

I tore my eyes from the bloody gauze and focused on Edna's grandmotherly face. "My mother was—"

Ashe squeezed my hand firmly, which I took for a shut-up signal. "Long story, best left for after lunch," he said.

"Not a lot of DBDs to choose from right now. We don't get many diners down here this time of day. But there's always an oddball or two." She winked at Ashe then scanned us from head to toe. "Y'all look plumb awful."

"Gee, thanks."

"What happened?"

"Edna..."

"Sorry, I know better than to ask questions. Anyway, I have showers and a couple of rooms y'all can snooze in. Now what will it be? I got a nice O neg here right now."

"I don't know. Sounds pricey," Ashe said, rubbing his chin like he was trying to decide between a sirloin and filet mignon.

"Lunch special. Half off."

"Sounds good. Let's get Wren a sample."

Edna nodded and called out to a woman seated across the room who was sipping a drink and flipping through a magazine. "Harriet, lunch special and a sample, please. Table six."

Harriet was tall and muscular, with bright red hair and pale skin turned nearly brown from freckles. She wore jean shorts, flip flops, and a long-sleeved plaid flannel shirt with a tank top underneath, all a size too small. She tossed the magazine on the table and put down her drink – it looked purplish like the iron supplement in the back hallway, and smelled like fake raspberry too.

Edna ushered us to a table, where Ashe and I sat close to each other. Zac sat on the edge of his seat at a nearby table, his chair facing us, still looking around with those intense dark eyes as though Dracula might emerge at any moment.

Harriet sat opposite us at our table, smiled, and nodded at me and Ashe in turn. "I assume your girlfriend here's getting the sample."

"Yes, please," Ashe said. "If that's okay with you, Wren?"

I nodded, not certain what I was okay with, but if it involved a fresh meal of blood, I was totally down with that.

Edna returned to the table carrying a tray. On the tray sat an empty clear plastic cup, along with a clean scalpel and gauze pads, and a bottle of rubbing alcohol. Harriet removed her flannel shirt and draped it over the back of her chair. Edna soaked a gauze pad with alcohol and wiped Harriet's wrist. Then she held the woman's wrist over the cup and made a small slice across an artery with the scalpel. Fresh, bright-red blood flowed from the wound. Edna set the scalpel on the tray and flipped Harriet's wrist upside down. Blood poured into the cup. Steam condensed on the inside of the cup as the blood level rose.

All this time, Harriet was casually looking off in the distance as though it didn't bother her in the least.

My mouth watered as I watched the hot blood pour into the cup. I could hear Harriet's pulse, calm and steady, saw how the tiny area of skin at her wrist above the cut rose and fell with every heartbeat. I didn't know how long I could control the urge to sink my fangs into her arm.

"You got your papers, ma'am?" Harriet asked.

"What?" I forced my eyes to leave the visual feast of her fresh blood and met Harriet's calm gaze.

"Your papers. You can drink from prepackaged, but you need papers to get a meal from the source."

Ashe put his hand on my thigh as if to calm me down, but it sent electrical pulses straight to my core. At least it was enough to snap me out of beast mode for a moment. I turned to meet his copper-eyed gaze. His eyes were even more beautiful in this light. I wouldn't feel the least bit uncomfortable staring right into those gems while he fucked me.

"Wren, papers mean you're free of communicable diseases. Have you got anything like that?"

I shook my head, mesmerized by the way his lips slid over his slightly emerged fangs as he spoke.

"Your doctor could print them for you."

"What doctor?" I blinked, averting my gaze to somewhere less dangerous, like Zac's crotch. Shit, no. Uh, where to look? There, by a door across the room – a framed quote from Marilyn Monroe: *Dogs never bite me, just humans*. Weirdly appropriate, but better.

"You don't have a doctor?"

I slumped in the seat, laughing sarcastically. "Oh, sure, I've had lots of them. They're delicious."

He squeezed his eyes shut with a half smile. "Seriously, Wren?"

I sat up straight and rested my hand on *his* thigh. His whole body tensed. Good. Served him right. "Yeah, seriously. I don't even know what a DBD is."

Edna answered without looking up from the bloodletting. "Designated Blood Donor."

"Yeah, okay, whatever. None of this – the DBDs, the prison, my mother being a queen of something. I don't know shit from shinola."

Edna and Harriet both snapped to attention, wide-eyed.

"It's from an old movie," I added. "*The Jerk*. Steve Martin. No?" Apparently my area of expertise lay in old music, movies, and TV shows. Yeah, that'd be a real help.

Ashe squeezed my thigh, glancing at them before he held me in a cold copper stare. "Listen, I know you want answers, and you will get them, but not here, not now. Priorities first. We get you fed, rested, and somewhere we'll both be safe. Just be patient."

"She's hungry. Be patient with *her*," Zac said.

Ashe sat back in his chair, removed his hand from my thigh, and held up both hands in brief surrender. "Sorry."

"Okay, hon. Try this." Edna set the cup of fresh blood in front of me. She held gauze over Harriet's wrist.

Ashe wiped his thumb with alcohol and bit the tip of it. Edna removed the gauze from Harriet's wrist as Ashe smeared his blood onto the wound. It closed almost immediately.

Edna quickly wiped the leftover blood from Harriet's skin then looked at me. "Drink it before it gets cold, hon."

She didn't have to tell me twice. I snatched up the blood and drank it down, savoring the rich, hot, iron-filled goodness as it slid down my throat and eased my growling stomach. I slammed down the cup and wiped my mouth with a napkin.

"Well?" Ashe asked.

"That was amazing. Can I have more? Please?"

"Of course, hon. I've got a whole pint in the kitchen back there. I'll warm it up for you and bring it out." Ashe started to protest, but Edna smiled. "It's on the house. Poor girl's starving."

Zac groaned and stood from his chair. "I don't think I can watch any more of this."

Edna chuckled. "Okay, then come with me. I'll point you to the diner upstairs."

Edna took Harriet's other wrist and quickly wiped it with alcohol before hurrying to another room with a swinging door, which I assumed was the vampire kitchen. Zac followed her, glancing back at me and Ashe with a frown before he slipped through the door.

Ashe scooted closer to Harriet, picked up her wrist and brought it to his mouth. Her eyes widened slightly as his fangs emerged. He pierced her skin, slowly sinking the sharp tips deeper into her flesh until his lips were seated fully over her artery. Her breath hitched. She made a fist and tightened it, then loosened it in the rhythm of a slow, steady heartbeat.

I watched his chin and Adam's apple moving up and down, heard the gentle slurping as a tiny stream escaped the corner of his mouth. I wiped it from her arm before it dripped on him and licked my finger. He raised his gaze to mine, his mouth curving briefly into a smile. Yellow light from the table lamp flickered like dancing flames in his copper eyes.

Harriet closed her eyes and let out a quiet moan. Her body gravitated closer to him. She gripped the hem of her shirt as though she had to resist touching him.

I was getting wet just watching Ashe have lunch. I'd never been so turned on by eating before. I mean, who gets turned on by rats and dying homeless people? I made a mental note to find a vampire phone book and get a vampire doctor appointment ASAP.

Edna emerged from the kitchen with a blood donor bag shaped like a juice pouch with a straw in one end. "Here ya' go, hon. Drink up."

"Thank you." I took the pouch from her and sipped. It was good, but like the equivalent of a frozen pizza compared to a homemade one. I sat back in my chair and watched my insta-boyfriend drink blood from a willing human in an oddly sensual dining experience.

HARRIET'S SHIFT ENDED, so she left just as Zac reemerged from the kitchen. He looked more satisfied and smelled more like barbeque than body odor.

"How was it?" we asked each other at the same time.

I laughed. "Good, and yours?"

"Extra greasy, but nothing some Tums can't handle."

Now that we were all full, I could finally take account of how bad we looked and smelled. But I had so many things to ask now that my brain wasn't fogged over with hunger.

"How about a shower and a good nap?" Ashe asked as though reading my mind. "We can talk more tonight."

"Okay."

Zac cleared his throat. "I'll ditch the van and come back with your car. I think we should get on the road as soon as the sun sets, so that'll be about...." He consulted his mobile phone. "Eight-thirty. You have plenty of time to rest up and whatever."

He grimaced at the word *whatever* as though imagining Ashe and me in the throes of passion.

"Okay, be careful out there," I said.

"Sure. Be careful in here, too." He tossed Ashe a cold glare and left the way we had entered.

Surely the detective wasn't jealous. I found that quite hilarious. Like I was the Bella for their Edward and Jacob testosterone competition. I'd always thought such a triangle was ridiculous, but I could understand the ego trip. If they decided to brawl over me, I'd insist they do it without teeth or weapons. And without clothes. With lots of oil.

As soon as Zac's footsteps faded down the hall, Ashe stood and ran a hand through his sandy blond hair. "So...what now?"

"So..." I slowly stood, wondering the same thing. Shower and sleep were a given, but a lot could happen in a few hours. "I think you owe me a kiss."

CHAPTER EIGHT

ASHE

DAMN RIGHT, I OWED Wren a kiss. More than one, all over her pouty lips, and then I'd skip straight to the good stuff and kiss up the insides of her thighs. What would she taste like, feel like when I sank inside her? I got hard just thinking about it. Harder, actually, if that were even possible. I'd sported a chub since I'd first laid eyes on her. Now, as I pushed to my feet to stand next to her, watching her eye-fuck me, I was sure I wore the same expression she did while my dick strained against the zipper of my prison uniform underneath the guard's uniform.

"I just realized I have on entirely too many clothes," I said.

She lifted an eyebrow. "We should probably find a solution for that. Like a shower?"

Check, please. A low rumble started deep in my chest. "Only if you'll join me."

She grinned, and it was all I could do not to throw her down on the table right here. "I did say you owed me a kiss."

Still spinning from my insane day, I just about went into a tailspin when I took her hand and hauled balls out of the DBD feeding area. Her touch charged a lightning storm through my skin, reminding me that I was here, and free, because of her. It had been stressful as hell to get to this point, but it was so worth it.

She turned to me, and her grin grew wider, even more gorgeous, fueling my need to kiss her, taste her, be inside her right now.

In the same wood-paneled hallway we'd come in through, I released her hand to push her back against the wall. Roughly, I tilted her head back and covered her mouth with mine, groaning when I could still taste the blood she'd drunk on her lips.

She arched into me, her arms wrapping to the back of my head, her chest pressed against mine. Her lips and tongue matched my intensity, and soft moans rumbled into me and then all the way down to my dick. Then, she rolled her hips into mine, and I just about lost it right there. With a growl, I wrapped my arms around to her ass to grind her up against me. She felt so good, so soft, yet unbreakable too. I wouldn't have to be gentle with her. Her legs wrapped around my waist, and she used the wall as leverage to dry hump me.

Sweet vampire Jesus, why were we still wearing clothes?

I set her on her feet and pulled away, drunk with lust and blood and freedom and adrenaline. We needed to get to a room. Wren took my hand, her lips swollen with my kisses, eyes bright with hunger, her guard's uniform top sliding down to reveal her bare shoulder. Fuck it. Who needed a room when the hallway would work just fine?

With a laugh, she sidestepped my advance to just take her right here and pointed to a door marked Bathroom. "I'll wash your back if you wash mine?"

I groaned low in my throat because I was pretty sure I'd warped back to caveman days and had lost the ability to form words. Female, good. Naked female, gooder.

I followed her in, just barely noticing the blue-tiled floor, the cinder block partition between the restrooms and sinks on one side and the showers on the other, and the low, wooden benches. We headed toward the showers, still clothed, damn it. From the sound of things, we were alone in here, but thankfully the showers were partitioned and curtained.

Wren turned on the water, and I stepped underneath the spray, both of us still fully clothed. I'd worry about that in a bit. More, uh, pressing matters took up my brain capacity. The shock of cold did nothing to cool me down. I wrapped my arms around to her front and kissed the back of her neck while she fiddled with the temperature.

"I think the lever is broken," she said.

I groaned into her creamy skin. "It's really not."

Her laugh turned into a moan when I skimmed my hand down her stomach to rub her through her two pairs of pants. She melted against me, leaning her head against my chest and pressing her ass to my straining dick. I slid my hands back up underneath her shirts as she arched her neck to give me better access to the soft skin around her collarbone. She tasted like heat and sex, all wrapped up into a tight, gorgeous package. I ridded her of both shirts, and she turned in my arms to help me with mine.

Like a magnet, my mouth found hers again with enough force to push us both back under the water. It soaked our lips and tongues but made me even thirstier. My hands roamed everywhere over her body, needing to get her out of her bra and pants but also to squeeze her tighter against me at the same time.

She peeled both my guard and prisoner shirts off of me and then ran her hands down my chest, following the streams of water until her fingers rested on the waist of my pants.

Over the sound of the water, a pop rang out. Loud and close enough to separate us. We looked at each other, both of us seeming unsure and very much wanting to go back to what we'd been doing.

Wren licked her lips and glanced down at my dick pressing painfully against my soaked, too-tight pants. "That pop wasn't you."

"No." I stepped in closer, telling myself to hell with whatever that sound was. "It definitely wasn't."

She grinned, and I lifted my hand to her face to wipe a wet piece of platinum hair from her forehead when there was a loud bang. It sounded like the bathroom door bursting open.

Both of us jumped and stared out through the curtain as if we could see anything behind its cream opaqueness. The air in the bathroom changed, not just the hot steam escaping through the open door but also the sense that we weren't alone. And three was definitely a crowd.

Was that Zac? I leaned against the wall of the shower stall and peered out through a crack in the curtain. A shadow moved along the floor, moving toward the toilet side of the bathroom first even though our shower was obviously on. Making sure that side was empty before they came for the naked shower people, no doubt. But we weren't nearly as naked as I wanted to be. A bad thing under normal circumstances. A good thing if this person was trouble though. Maybe they just really needed to piss.

I turned back to Wren who was peeking out the other side of the curtain. She shot her arm out to catch mine and squeezed, her body tense. A warning. Shit. I needed a weapon, anything to get us out of here. My options were a cracked green bar of soap someone had left in the tray in the wall, and an empty travel-sized bottle of hair conditioner.

Awesome. Why did survival lately feel like a test I didn't study for?

The curtain fluttered, and not because of us. Someone was coming, and not the happy kind either. I had the element of surprise in that I knew they were here, but I doubted that would be enough to get us out.

Keeping my eyes glued to the fluttering curtain, I pushed Wren back against the wall opposite mine, out of the way, I hoped. I waited, my whole body coiled tight. Then, when a slight shadow darkened the curtain, I took the spraying shower head and wrenched it out of the wall.

The curtain snapped open, and a vampire I'd never seen before wearing black ops gear stood there with his silver bullet gun already aimed.

Wren jumped at him. Shirtless, soaking wet, and sexy as fuck, she knocked the gun from his hand and immediately followed that with a wicked left hook that looked like it really rang his bell.

I stood there like an idiot with a shower head in my hands. Water gushed from the hole in the wall behind me and seeped out onto the blue-tiled floor around Wren's boots and the vampire she was currently punching holes in. And the similarly dressed guy creeping around the bathroom's divide behind Wren's shoulder.

So, I would get to use the shower head after all. Things were really looking up these days.

The creeping guy lifted his gun at Wren's back. I shot out of the stall, my shoes slipping along the wet tiles, and collided with him. The butt of his gun slammed into my jaw so hard I spun into the wall face-first. I bounced back before I fully recovered my senses, and the guy hit me again in the exact same place.

Pain exploded, times two. *Fucker*.

I went down with a splash in the already inch-deep water, feeling every single tile as I hit.

"Ashe!" Wren shouted behind me.

"Leave him alive!" the other vampire shouted at the exact same time.

Me. He was talking about *me*. They wanted me back in jail, alive, but they didn't look like police.

Wren cried out, but I didn't see what happened. I was too busy staring down the barrel of the gun pointed at my head by the guy who'd hit me.

"Drop your weapon," he ordered.

Fuck that. I'd destroyed some perfectly good property to get this shower head. I lifted my free hand in surrender, released one end of the shower head, and slowly moved like I was going to put the rest of it down too.

Then I flashed it out toward his gun so it jerked the barrel away. He fired. Tile exploded right by my head, but I was already surging to my feet before he could aim again. I crashed the shower head into his nose, then punched him in the ribs, then in the nose again, the same exact spot. Ha! Blood squirted, and he tripped over the water onto his ass.

Movement blurred at my side, and I started to swing, but I caught myself. It was Wren, looking mighty pissed, her face cut and bruised but still just as gorgeous as ever. She splashed toward the vamp, who scrambled for his gun that he must've dropped. I kicked it out of his reach and then picked it up.

"Who are you?" I demanded and pointed his own gun at him.

Before he could answer, though, Wren circled to his back, put him in a choke hold, and squeezed until a loud crack echoed around the bathroom. She let out a wild battle cry as his head came clean off. Then she tossed it aside like it was a bad coconut and skipped back as his body slumped to the floor. Blood spattered the tiles around the twitching vampire.

I blinked. I'd never actually seen someone do that before.

Wren stood, her face hard and unflinching as if she did this every day. It was a different expression than when she'd busted me out of jail. Either that, or I was an entirely altered person, seeing her from a brand new, darker perspective now that she wasn't dangling my own freedom in front of me.

She flicked her gaze to me, and her face softened. "I probably should've waited to do that until after you got your answer, huh?"

"Yeah," was all I could say.

"I usually have no interest in what they have to say."

Usually. I glanced behind me at the other pile of dead and headless corpses. Never mind these vampires. Who was *Wren*? This was the second time today she'd left a trail of bodies. *Was* this something she did every day? While a small, I-need-serious-therapy part of me thought it was kind of hot, another small part of me wondered if maybe I'd be better off in jail. She'd dragged me into a killing war I wanted no part of, even if one side was gunning for *me*. Though, yeah, to be fair, she'd also dragged me away from jail. I needed to push aside the rush my sudden freedom gave me, tell my dick to behave, and then have a sit-down with Wren to see if she'd eventually kill me too. Just because she'd set me free didn't mean I could trust her. Or fuck her in the shower.

This was what I got for thinking with my dick. My freed dick, at least in the figurative sense. Almost literally too.

A surprised cry sounded from somewhere nearby, and I had a feeling we would have more company if we planted ourselves here for too much longer. I crossed toward the open door and pressed my back against it to peer out, aiming the gun I'd stolen at the ground. Farther down the hallway, trickles of blood spread over the floor from the dining room.

Shit.

"There's nowhere to go," Wren whispered behind me.

She was right. The sun was still up, which meant the vampires had black op'd their way in...somehow. Unless Zac had come back with some wheels, we were stuck. Unless Wren sicced herself on all of them, and I'd rather she didn't. Just because I'd planned a murder I'd never carried out didn't mean I was a big fan of killing.

"Come on." I took her hand and pulled her out of the bathroom. We could hole up somewhere, maybe capture another of those vampires and get him to talk.

My and Wren's wet feet slapped the floor, punctuated with a steady *dripdripdrip* off the few clothes we wore. We were leaving a wet trail right to us. I hadn't seen any towels in the bathroom, but I did remember seeing some napkins in boxes near the shelves by the stairs. Better than nothing. We headed in that direction.

I handed her a package of napkins, then pushed her inside a small broom closet, flicked the light on, and left the door open just a crack to hear if we were about to be ambushed.

"Take off your clothes," I said, simultaneously hating and loving the sound of those words.

"Only if you say that exact same thing to me later." She grinned and leaned over to peel her wet pants down her hips, giving me quite the eyeful of perfect cleavage contained in her black lace bra. Smooth legs climbed a long, long way up to matching panties. She gave a little shake of her ass when her pants snagged on her foot.

Vampire Jesus, help me. I tore my eyes away and somehow got both pairs of soggy pants down over my boxers and raging boner, at least the third I'd had today, all in the short time I'd known Wren. If we weren't constantly running, I could go somewhere and deal with it on my own before I drilled Wren. *Grilled* Wren. Grilled. Had a discussion.

Fuck.

Through the crack in the door, another armed vampire passed, dressed similar to the two in the shower.

Wren, without any sound, started to spring out after him, but I caught her elbow, spun her around, and covered her mouth before she could protest.

"You don't have to kill everyone, Wren," I hissed.

She flinched as if I'd struck her, and I hated the way she was looking at me now, with hurt and a little revulsion, exactly how Jessica had looked at Devin that night. That look dropped my gut to my knees, especially since I'd put it there. But Wren *didn't* need to kill everyone. She needed to know that. Or maybe she did know that and didn't care.

Her face contorted with anger, and she ripped my hand from her mouth. "They're after you, Ashe. You want me to just let them take you?"

"No, I want you to let me question them."

She waved her hand at the door. "Then let's go."

"Fine. Let me take the lead on this so I can get answers."

She studied me for a long moment. "You don't trust me."

"I don't know you. I don't know anything about you."

Her eyes narrowed as she threw her pants at me, the wet fabric like a slap. "Where was all this distrust in the shower when your hands were down my pants, Ashe?"

"A moment of weakness." One of many to come, I was sure, especially since she was mostly naked.

"Well. Thanks for that," she said, her voice sharp enough to stake me through the heart.

She stormed out, and it was then I realized she didn't steal one of the vampire's guns. She didn't need one. She was just as lethal, if not more.

I followed on her heels, our clothes wedged under my elbow and my gun pointed down. As soon as I cleared the broom closet door, the exit door to my left opened. Sunlight angled through, and I dove to one side of the hallway to avoid it. It couldn't be a vampire coming in, but I tried to look as innocent as possible anyway, as much as a mostly naked escaped prisoner can look innocent.

The door swung shut, and I could finally see again.

Zac trotted down the steps, swinging a ring of keys around his finger. He stopped when he saw me, naked except for my boxers, then flicked his gaze to Wren farther up the hallway. She looked over her shoulder at him.

His gaze darkened when he saw the firm line of her lips, how she was moving away from me while wearing next to nothing, instead of toward me. Instead of on top of me. I could guess how this looked. Shit.

Zac slammed me into the wall with an accusing finger pointed at my face. "What did you do to her?"

Shaking her head, Wren continued down the hallway. "I saved his life, and he got all twitchy about it. Leave him alone, Zac."

I shoved Zac off of me. "Yeah, leave me alone, Zac. We need to get out—"

A safety clicked off from the direction of Wren as loud as a cannon. A fourth person had joined our hallway party, in front of Wren, his gun pointed right at her head.

I dropped the wet clothes and stepped closer, my gun lifted. "Drop your gun."

"He's here," the vampire shouted.

He being me. *Fuck*.

"Zac, we need to get out of here. Go make that happen. Now!" I shouted.

"I'll get the car and pull it up to the door," Zac said, his voice low, and sprinted back up the steps. The door opened, but I was far enough away from the sun this time.

Wren's hands curled at her sides as she stared the vampire down, and I could guess exactly what she was thinking.

I took a step toward her and the vampire, my skin itching to get the hell out of here.

The guy narrowed his eyes at Wren. "Are you related to the queen?"

In a blur of movement, she knocked the gun out of his hands, twirled it around, and pointed it at him. "Who sent you?"

The guy went through all five stages of grief at the loss of his gun within seconds. "The queen herself. Seems like she's got her eye on that one." He nodded toward me.

Queen Ravana? Because I was accused of killing her sister, Bronwen, both of whom looked so much like Wren? What the hell did all of this have to do with me since I didn't kill Bronwen? Pretty sure I'd remember doing that since I couldn't even kill my own sister's ex-boyfriend.

A car honked loudly from just outside.

"Wren!" I shouted.

She backed toward me quickly as the sounds of the other men—or women; both genders were equally pissed at me—closed in.

Then she turned and ran toward me. We took the stairs three at a time and burst through the door out into the daylight. Immediately the sun beat down on our naked skin in painful waves. An open trunk of a turquoise classic car waited for us. We threw ourselves in and slammed it shut.

"Fuck my life," I said into the dark interior of the trunk.

We squealed away from Edna's Itchen.

But I was so tired of running away lately. It was high time I started running toward some answers.

CHAPTER NINE

WREN

YOU DON'T NEED TO kill everyone, *Wren.* The words banged around in my head, drawing out shards of shame and guilt that I really didn't need right now. My whole life had been dedicated to eradicating my mother's killers by whatever means necessary. There was no room for anything so hindering as guilt.

It didn't help that Zac was driving Birdie like some drunk Nascar driver along roads that needed serious attention. Being stuck back here in a trunk with a vampire who didn't trust me while a human was fucking up my paint job was not my idea of a fabulous day.

It also didn't help that we'd landed in the trunk so that my head was crammed against my guitar case and Ashe was spooned up against my back. Every bump made it feel like he was dry humping me. Or damp humping me since we were both in wet underwear and nothing more. We couldn't do it even if we wanted to – and wanted to, we certainly did – but a '59 Thunderbird isn't known for its trunk space. It was tight as a coffin in there and kind of felt like one with the quilted lining I'd added to cover the bare metal and spare tire, among other things.

"Wren." Ashe's gentle whisper made me flinch. I wasn't used to hiding with anyone but my mother, and that had been a long time ago.

"Who ratted us out?" I asked, the question sounding as bitter as the blood that lingered in the back of my throat.

"I don't know. Maybe they followed us or Zac. Or..." He hesitated, groaning quietly as though he didn't want to speak the truth.

"Or what?"

"It might have been Edna."

"Edna? I thought she was on your side?"

"She is, I think, but she probably doesn't have much choice in the matter."

"What do you mean? Like she *has* to turn you in?"

"Uh, yeah, but it's complicated. We should discuss it later."

"Later? No, it's already been later. It's time for now." As much as I could, stuck in a not-very-well-padded trunk while lying on a spare tire, I flipped around until I could face Ashe. By then, my eyes had adjusted from the bright flare of sunshine that had blinded me before we became undead luggage. I could see his face like a cool blue night vision camera. In his eyes, though I couldn't see their copper color, I could clearly detect apprehension in his unblinking stare.

"Wren, I don't think—"

"I don't care what you think. Who was my mother?"

He finally blinked, squeezing his eyes shut for a moment before opening them and not quite meeting my gaze. "She was the queen of the Southern clan of the Vampire Nation."

My jaw trembled from an involuntary shiver. "Which means?"

"She ruled over all vampires from Texas to West Virginia, about fourteen or fifteen different states."

"Ruled? As in an actual monarch?" I hated feeling so ignorant, like I'd been living in a hole in the ground, only now emerging to find that the real world was much more complicated than I had imagined. I didn't currently own a TV, didn't keep up with the news. All I did was sing on stage and track down my mother's killers. My mother. A damn queen.

"Kind of. It's a matriarchal system. Her mother was queen, and her grandmother before that. Which means..."

"What? That I should be queen?"

"Well, yeah, if anyone actually knew you existed. But your mother acted more like a president, unlike those before her, putting more power into the hands of governors and representatives from each state who could vote on various things. It had pretty much been a monarchy before. She was determined to lead us into a democracy."

"So, is there no queen currently?"

"Uh, yeah there is, actually. Your mother's sister, the next in line. After you, of course."

"And her name?"

"Ravana."

The name chilled my skin like icy fingers racing down my spine. I'd heard that name before, at the jail, but somewhere else too... A distant phone rang in the recesses of my memory. It was daytime. We were supposed to be asleep in the basement of a funeral home. I wanted to try sleeping in a coffin like Lestat. It looked so comfy in the movies. In reality, it wasn't as padded as it looked and smelled weird, like moth balls and varnish and the kind of synthetic plastic that makes you wrinkle your nose in the Walmart shoe section.

My mother hated coffins. Claustrophobia, probably, so she would sleep beside me on the floor. I remembered lifting the lid just a teensy bit, enough to peek through a tiny slit of daylight that filtered in through a humidity-fogged window overhead. She was standing by a phone mounted on the wall. Her white-knuckled fingers gripped the cord, wound it round and round her knuckles, one after the other. She spoke in a panicked whisper, upset with whoever was on the other line.

"He can't be. Are you sure?" She leaned her back against the concrete block wall, covering her mouth to choke back a sob. "There's no hope, then. Wren can't fight her, not without them." A pause, then she glanced toward my coffin but must not have noticed the tiny space I spied her through. "She's too young. She'll never make it." Another pause, before her normally kind, soft eyes flared red with rage I'd never seen before. "Keep the rest of them alive. I don't care what you have to do. I'll make sure Wren is nowhere near them. Ravana can't find them before they're mated."

I must have been saying that out loud, because Ashe's hand was on my shoulder, shaking me.

"You remember her? Your aunt, I mean?"

I shook my head. "Never met her. I only remember my mother mentioning her name that one time. I had no idea who she was talking about. I remember asking her what was wrong, but as usual, she brushed me off and told me not to worry about it. But what did she mean by keeping me away from them? Who's *them*? And before they're mated? What the fuck does that mean?"

"I'm not entirely sure, but you know the symbols on our arms?"

I held up my wrist, where the pink circle with one blue star-point spoke still glowed with a comfortable, warm light.

"I think there's more to that symbol, as in, I don't think it's complete."

Then came the clueless slow blink as I tried to make sense of what he was saying. My brain had flatlined. "I don't follow."

He smiled and cupped my cheek, stroking my skin with his thumb. The same heat and ache built at my core as it had in the shower, but then he pulled back suddenly as if he remembered what had happened after our shower.

You don't need to kill everyone, Wren.

"Like all queens before her, your mother had five bonded mates," he said.

"What, like a male harem?"

"Yeah. I...think it's supposed to be the same for you."

"You're supposed to be my mate."

There was a long pause—too long—while his expression blanked. "Yes."

He certainly seemed excited about it. Was I? The hell if I knew. This was too much to process.

Mates. Five of them. "Then that means..."

He nodded. "There are four more guys out there dying to get into your pants."

MY SECOND SHOWER OF the day was much less exciting than the first. Either the budget hotel we'd wound up in had installed a low-flow shower head, or it needed some serious unclogging. Three streams spit water that couldn't decide if they wanted to be hot or cold, alternately freezing and burning me. The vinyl shower curtain was spotted with mildew. Stale vomit odor blew up from the A/C vent every time the cool air kicked on.

Legs still aching from being crammed into a coffin-trunk, I turned off the water and wobbled out of the tub. The men were arguing on the other side of the door.

"Yeah, and what's your plan, big man? Keep hopping from one ratty hotel to another until what?" Ashe demanded.

"Until we find answers!" Zac shouted back.

I toweled off, feeling more like a mother to two testosterone-fueled teenagers than a queen in hiding. A queen. Me? It still didn't make sense. Nothing in my life had been tea-and-crumpets comfortable. Then there was the issue of five, count 'em, *five* mates. I towel dried my hair and ran my fingers through the damp platinum strands. In the mirror, I looked nothing like a queen, just a pale, tattooed woman with yellow-orange eyes who looked a little too bony from having lived mostly on rats and dying humans, only some of whom I'd actually wanted to kill.

"Oh really, and what are the questions?" Ashe's voice rumbled with a distinct growl that meant trouble if I didn't intervene.

So I did. I opened the door and strode through the room over to the curtain-covered window. I peeked out. The sun hadn't set yet, but a rainstorm had moved in, so the daylight was tolerable.

"Well?" I asked. "What *are* the questions?"

I looked over my shoulder with a half smile at the men who had now gone dead quiet, their eyes as big as Moon Pies, staring at my bare ass.

"Uh..." Zac shook himself out of his trance and turned away, digging through his bag that sat on one of the beds. "The main question is who killed Queen Bronwen, and why? There are plenty of other questions, but I think those will lead us to her killers. Wren's taken care of some of them already."

"How many more can there be?" Outside, a hunch-backed old man leaned on the railing that surrounded the walkway of the hotel's second story. He stuck a cigarette in his mouth, cupped his hand over it, and tried to light it. Was that a signal of some sort? I couldn't let myself be paranoid over every stranger that crossed our path. Chances are he knew nothing about vampires. But in any case, we couldn't linger here for long.

Ashe groaned and blurred himself into the bathroom, slamming the door behind him.

I chuckled and turned in time to catch a wad of clothes Zac threw at me.

He shook his head, grinning. "You're evil."

"Vampire. Whatcha gonna do?" I tossed the clothes on the bed. A hot pink bra and panties—both sheer—were bundled in the middle of a racerback black tank top and black leggings. "Pink's really not my color."

"Only thing they had at Walmart."

"Yeah, right. But...thanks for getting me clothes and rescuing us and all that." The underwear Ashe and I still wore when we arrived at the hotel were now dry but crusted with dried blood. Zac must have gotten the leggings and tank when he was out fetching my car. I had a few changes of clothes hidden in my trunk which I'd forgotten to bring inside, but he wouldn't have known that unless he searched the car.

I still didn't know how fully I could trust him, or Ashe for that matter. The past couple of days had completely scrambled my brain. I'd thought my original life goal of tracking down and killing my mother's killers was hard. Compared to what I'd just learned about my origins, that had been a piece of cake.

"Sure." He glanced at me then averted his eyes again. "How about you put them on?"

"Okay, if you insist."

As I pulled off the tags and put the decidedly scratchy bra on, Zac cleared his throat.

"Your car stands out too much," he said.

"Birdie? Yeah, so?"

"We're going to need to ditch it for something less conspicuous."

I slipped on the panties. Yep, also scratchy. "That's a no from me."

"Wren, I'm serious."

"Fine. I'll take care of it." I slipped on the shirt and sat on the bed to put on the leggings.

"What?" Zac slowly turned his eyes toward me, his shoulders relaxing when he found me clothed. Then he was back to serious bodyguard mode. "You can't just steal a car. We already have enough trouble following us."

I laughed. "How little you know me." I went to the window and looked out. The rain had stopped. Zac had parked Birdie behind the hotel, backed between a dumpster and the building so no one could see the car from the road. It should give me enough cover to do what had to be done.

"Stay here." I went to the bathroom, where steam rolled out from beneath the closed door. The shower was running. I turned the knob, which was unlocked. Inside, I grabbed a clean towel and started to leave, but the temptation was too much.

Pulling back the edge of the shower curtain just enough to peek in, I saw Ashe, one hand supporting himself on the tile in front of him, head down, the water pounding his hair, cascading down his back, over his firm ass and muscled legs. His other arm moved in front of him with quick stroking motions.

Everything in me wanted to join him.

He sagged forward, his fingers digging into the tile, while his low groan vibrated the air in a direct path between my thighs.

Breathless, I licked my lips, squeezed my legs together at the sight of him. He seemed so vulnerable in that moment.

Then he opened his mouth.

"Watching me jack off now? You could have been nice and took care of it for me, or are blowjobs beneath a queen?" He looked over his shoulder and gave me a hard stare.

His words bit into me, froze the heat between my legs. I turned and left the bathroom, but not before having the last word. "Guess you'll never know now, asshole."

CHAPTER TEN

ASHE

I SLAMMED MY FIST into the shower tiles, spreading a web of cracks around the indentation and splitting my knuckles. Why was I such a piece of shit sometimes? I was exhausted, beyond sexually frustrated even though I'd just jerked myself off, and confused at the new directions my life was pulling me in lately. Still, I'd hurt Wren just now. No, not just now but before at Edna's Itchen too. The look she gave me after I'd hurt her felt like a splintered stake twisted into my heart. I didn't want to hurt her anymore. Ever. I just wanted answers.

I just wanted *her*. She'd watched me in here, her eyes scorched with hunger and her tongue sliding over her plump lips. Lips I'd tasted. Lips that drove me insane. Had she known I'd been thinking about her while I'd stroked myself? Her mouth, her soft curves pressed against my body, the smell of her skin...

And...I was hard again already. Fuck my life.

After I turned the water off—well, slowed it to a trickle; off in this hotel was relative—I quickly stepped out, toweled off, and dressed in the clothes Zac had bought.

Baggy pants, a too-small shirt with Bite Me printed on it, and a baseball cap. Seriously? Chin Dimple sure had a wicked sense of humor.

I needed to go after Wren and apologize. So what if she was a killing machine? I wasn't exactly faring well in the morals department either. Maybe that was why we were meant to be together—because we would both do whatever it took to sever the crown from the queen and place it on its rightful owner's head.

This was some pretty heavy shit for an innocent fugitive with a massive hard-on.

Even though the minor cuts on my knuckles had sealed over with my healing power, I grabbed a towel and pressed it to my hand so it would hang strategically over my crotch. Then I opened the door to a wall of pissed-off human named Zac.

He stuck his finger into my face, close enough that if I shifted slightly, he could pick my nose. "What the fuck did you do? She just stormed out of here."

"She *left*?"

"She's taking care of the car. It's too conspicuous," he said and lowered his finger. "Now what did you do?"

"Step off, man. It's been a wild day. I'm struggling to keep up and doing a terrible job of it..." When he didn't move, I shoved past him out of the bathroom. "Why did you guys break me out?"

He shrugged. "What else were we going to do today?"

"Uh-huh." I crossed to the window where I peered out through the curtains. Below, parked behind the hotel and blocked from the road by a dumpster was Wren's car. She leaned over it, her ass in the air and shaking a little as she dried it with a towel. I couldn't *not* look away.

Not when I was imagining myself right behind her, my fingers digging into her hips and sliding...

"...you've figured out who Wren's mom is?" Zac's voice drifted into my fantasy.

I ground my teeth together while the symbol on my wrist flared heat and spread it through my body. "Yeah. I know who Wren's mom is."

"Did Wren tell you she spent most of her life on the run with her mom until her mom was murdered?"

I glanced over my shoulder at him. "On the run from who?"

He shot me a look as if it should've been obvious. "Someone who didn't want Queen Bronwen to be queen anymore."

"Her sister, Queen Ravana?"

He nodded. "A group of thugs was hired to kill Wren's mom and were eventually successful. They caught her with a silver net and ended her life. And they did it in front of Wren."

My stomach lurched and sat too near my throat. I'd seen pictures of said silver net, shot inside my own apartment. "How old was Wren?"

"She said she was eight."

"Fuck." I sagged against the window, letting the curtain fall shut on my entire perception of Wren. She'd suffered through something unimaginable. An eight-year-old witnessing her mother's murder... How the hell did she find the will to go on after something like that? Or smile, which she had several times over the last twelve hours, each one more gorgeous than the last.

"Since then," Zac continued, "she raised herself, trained herself, and began to hunt her mother's killers down."

My muscles went rigid. Not the "killer" with a silver net found in his apartment with Bronwen's blood on it. Not the one accused of killing one of her five mates. What would Wren do when she found out about the net? She would kill me. Hell, *I* wanted to kill me, and I hadn't even done anything. Unless she did know... Unless Zac knew.

His gaze burned a hole into my spine, a crawling accusation pressing between each of my vertebrae.

Was that why they'd broken me out? Because they wanted to steal me away from the justice system so they could deliver their own vigilante brand?

I tensed. My ears straining to hear any sign of movement behind me, I turned to face him, slowly, attempting to appear normal when nothing would ever be again.

"Why did you break me out?" I asked again.

He half-assed a wave to my arm. "You've seen the symbol on your wrist, I take it?"

I fucking hated it when people answered my questions with another question. My fingers curled as I gave a short nod.

"That means you're important, a mate to the queen. The real queen..." A pained look briefly crossed his face.

"But...you're a human. Why do you care about who is or isn't the queen of the Southern Clan?"

He looked away, his hard expression telling me even less than his silence.

But he didn't appear like he was going to kill me. Yet. I had some severe trust issues, in case that wasn't obvious, but anyone would in this type of situation.

I pinched the bridge of my nose while I wished myself out of this situation. "I need to go tell Wren that I'm sorry."

"So you *were* a dick to her, then." He sat on the side of the bed and flashed me a glare.

I ignored him as I crossed to the room door, scooping up a room key card by the TV as I went, though still very much aware of him in case he made a wrong move.

"Think fast." He tossed something at me, and I plucked it easily out of the air.

A cell phone, one of those disposable prepaid ones, still sealed in that impossible-to-open plastic.

"Call the room phone if there's trouble." He lay back on the bed and closed his eyes. "Maybe I'll even answer."

Would a man who could be trying to kill me give me a phone? Probably not. I nodded to let that sink in a little farther into my thick skull.

"Thanks, man." I reached for the doorknob.

"Ashe," he said, his eyes still closed. "Leave the bloody towel here so you don't drop it like a jackass and leave DNA evidence of your whereabouts. And don't let her leave. I need... We need her alive so she can claim her rightful place."

I tossed the towel into the bathroom since my boner problem had long since gone, and then I left, making sure I had the key card and that the door locked behind me. Didn't want anyone to come and rough up Zac, now did we? He seemed entirely too vested in this mission, but what choice did I have other than following along?

My chances of survival alone were slim to none, and I wasn't about to leave Wren. Not now.

Down a long, carpeted hallway that smelled like a mix of chlorine and piss, I found an empty laundry room and ducked inside. Using my fangs, I tore open the plastic to get at the phone. Without fangs, I'd be fucked in the opening-sealed-plastic department. How did humans manage it? I accessed the motel's Wi-Fi, searched for my neighbor's number, and then dialed her up.

"Not interested, sick villain," she answered, as expected.

"Marta, it's Ashe."

"Still not interested, you pesky roughneck," she said.

I leaned against a dryer and rubbed my eyes hard enough to see sparks. Marta was my three-hundred-eighty-eight-year-old neighbor with papery frail skin, a collection of rare books that could rival the National Library of Vampires, and instantly hated anyone who dared to call her. The obvious solution would be to never answer the phone, but this was Marta, so it was best not to tell her that.

"Marta..." I forced a teasing note into my voice so she'd play nice.

"The Ashley I know would have never skipped Thursday bridge club," she said.

I sidestepped past the use of my given name, the sound of which dragged down my back like fingernails on a slate. Mom had named me that after a character in her favorite movie, *Gone With the Wind*. Not something I was particularly proud of. Instead, I focused on what day it was. Friday. Yesterday was bridge club, about the time I was being booked in jail for murdering my sister's ex-boyfriend I didn't kill.

"I'm so sorry," I said. "Something came up, something unavoidable."

"Uh-huh. Would it have anything to do with the police swarming your apartment and knocking on my door at all hours of the day?"

Shit. Deny, deny, deny, or admit I knew exactly what was going on?

"You can't fool me, Ashley Felix Jensen. I know every single thing about you, so before you lie to me, I told them you didn't do anything wrong. Not my handsome neighbor, no way. But if you even think about lying to me, I will call the police and accuse you myself of killing Mother Vampire Teresa."

I stifled a groan. "Pretty sure she's still alive."

"Don't you argue with me, boy. Now, did you do something against the law or not?"

"Yes, Marta, I did, but I didn't"—I looked around the laundry room and at the closed door to make sure no one eavesdropped—"kill anyone."

"That's my sweet Ashley. Of course you didn't. Now, why did I call you?"

"I called you, Marta, because I'd like to ask a favor. Can you tell Cussler that I need security tapes of our hallway for the last week?"

Cussler was our landlord. The police had probably already taken what he had, but I hoped he'd kept copies. If he did, the video might show who had snuck into my apartment to plant the bloody net used to kill Wren's mom. I lived on the tenth floor, so I suspected they'd come right in the front door.

Marta made a disgusted sound. "It's a good thing you're cute."

"Thank you for this, Marta. I owe you one."

"Then it's your turn to bring Bloody Marys to bridge club next week. And for every week after that."

I shook my head. "I'm not sure I can do that."

She was quiet for a long time, and I could practically hear her sadness reaching through the phone line and strangling my heart.

"You weren't very good at bridge anyway."

"No, I wasn't."

"But I liked you."

"Like, present tense. I'm not dead yet, Marta."

"Let's try to keep it that way, then. I'll talk to Cussler for you. Try not to do anything stupid." She hung up.

"I'll try not to," I said to the dial tone, and hung up too.

Even if I had a tape that proved the evidence was planted, that didn't really make a difference in terms of Devin's death. I had gone to the hotel to kill him, after all. Since he was already dead by the time I found him, at least one other person was trying to take him out. Maybe more if he was so paranoid that he'd worked up an immunity to silver.

So, if there was at least one other person who wanted him dead, then why hang his death, and Queen Bronwen's, on me? Why not that other guy who'd been there? Or girl. I hadn't actually seen their face, even when they'd staked me. They'd come from behind, and then vanished like a shadow with the flick of a light.

I rubbed my thumb over the symbol on my wrist, warm compared to the rest of my skin, and painful because Wren was too far away. She and Zac had found me because of the symbol I didn't know I had, but they had known. Other people might too. Other people like her aunt, Queen Ravana. But who else? Did my mother know? My father? They'd always been overprotective of Jessica and me when we were kids but then had started to loosen the strings...around the time that Queen Ravana took the throne. Because they thought both Wren's mom and Wren were dead? Or was this just a wild conspiracy my fried brain meat had cooked up?

Conspiracy or not, Queen Ravana wanted me, a part of the true queen's harem, locked up for good because I could help take her crown away. It was a good idea, but it would never work. Obviously, she had underestimated Wren, and me too. I would help Wren take her place on the throne. Not just because it was inked onto my wrist that we were meant to be together, but because it was the right thing to do for Wren after what she'd been through and because Ravana sucked balls as queen, and not in a good way either.

And yes, also because I wanted down Wren's pants. Hey, no one ever said I was perfect, but I did have a moral compass. It just got confused sometimes with magnetic...whatever. My undead heart was mostly in the right place, especially when it came to protecting those I loved.

Wasn't that exactly what Wren was doing? Yes. Yes, it was.

My throat constricted as I stared down at the phone. I wanted to call my sister, listen to her voice as she said whether she'd sent the police to her place to catch me or not, and then hear if she was telling the truth. A part of me didn't want to know if she could betray me like that, not after everything I'd almost done for her, like set out to kill a man. I didn't expect praise or any shit for that, but I just needed her to know that her safety and well-being meant everything to me. Seeing her broken that night from Devin's hands had unhinged me, rewired me to look out for my big sister when before, I would hold up both middle fingers high in the air so she'd be sure to see them from across a crowded room. I'd been such a typical little brother. Not anymore. Not ever again.

Finally, I just decided to text her something she'd be passionate enough about to text back an unknown number: *Win $5000 by texting your answer and the reason as a reply—are you Team Edward or Team Jacob?*

CHAPTER ELEVEN

WREN

THANKFULLY THE RAIN HAD cooled the air and loosened the humidity enough that my hair didn't stick to my face as I took care of Birdie. It did little to calm the storm brewing in my head. I concentrated on drying the car with the bath towel, almost risking moving at super speed in case the rain came again, but decided against it. I needed time with my thoughts, time to slow down. Eyes roamed over my ass from the direction of our room, and I could guess who they belonged to. I gave a little extra wiggle to drive him even more insane.

When I finished thoroughly drying the car, I pulled up the quilting in the trunk and grabbed a can of spray paint. After a good shake, I popped off the cap.

Ashe's voice startled me. "Don't do it, Wren. Not because you're mad at me."

"Don't flatter yourself."

"Look, I'm sorry, I didn't mean—"

"I didn't ask for any of this. I was doing fine on my own until Zac dragged me out here. To save *your* ass by the way."

I ventured a look at him. He wore a dark blue T-shirt screen-printed with a big yellow *Bite Me*. It was a little too small, which hugged his muscles nicely, but was too short and showed a line of pale skin above baggy blue athletic pants. He wore a baseball cap with an eagle on it low on his forehead, which shadowed his entire face.

"Zac got you some new clothes, too, huh?"

"Yeah, and they're not nearly as flattering as yours. I suspect he did that on purpose."

"You think?" I started spraying the black paint, wincing as it drowned out Birdie's beautiful peacock blue, which was officially called Indian Turquoise. Whatever it was, I hated hiding it.

He groaned. "This is painful to watch. Please don't do this to your car. We'll find another one."

Eyes closed briefly, I shook my head and then leveled a stare at Ashe. "Read it and weep, amateur."

I held up the can.

He pulled his gaze from mine and studied the label. "Plasti-Dip?"

"It's rubberized. Peels right off when you're ready to remove it. I'm not new at the whole hiding-out gig."

"Yeah, Zac filled me in on some of the details. How you survived and..." He went quiet while he studied me, really studied me, as if he were seeing me for the first time. "You're amazing."

"Stop trying to butter me up." I finished spraying the roof and started on the hood.

"I'm not," he said softly and stepped in close to me, his body right against mine.

I turned around and was immediately wrapped in his arms. At first, I went stiff. It wasn't a take-me-now kind of hug. It was something else entirely. Something that made me melt against him and lay my head on his shoulder. He smelled clean, mixed with his own distinct scent. I nuzzled my cheek against his jaw, breathing him in deep.

"You really are amazing, Wren."

"How so? Because I know how to disguise a car?"

"No, not that. Because you grew up alone as a kid and were able to survive long enough to become a kick-ass warrior queen."

I chuckled. It felt so strangely weird and wonderful to be held like this by a man who, while still a virtual stranger, had already forged a spot in my life. Sliding my arms around his waist, I raised my head and looked into his eyes. They really were a beautiful copper color, searching my face as though he wanted to memorize every feature.

Our lips came together like they were magnetized. He kissed me like no one else had before. Not rushed, but gentle and slow. Our tongues danced a delicate waltz together, tasting, teasing. I still desperately wanted him inside me. But this... It was like an incredible gourmet hors d'oeuvre, one that promised one hell of a good dinner very soon.

We reluctantly broke away from each other to continue Birdie's makeover. Ashe kept watch while I finished with the car. It was almost fully dark by then. We went back to the hotel room, where we found Zac fast asleep, sprawled sideways across the bed by his duffel bag. Poor guy, he was exhausted.

"How about we ditch He-Man for a little while and go someplace quiet?" Ashe whispered.

"What did you have in mind? This dump isn't my idea of romantic."

"I don't even know where we are for sure. Hard to get my bearings from a car trunk."

Zac's phone lay beside him on the bed. I picked it up silently, but of course, he had it locked with a code I hadn't learned yet. Luckily, there was a flyer on the dresser for a pizza delivery joint. On the back was a crude map, but it was enough to show me we were in a little town called Lil'Bit, Louisiana, and we were about a mile from the barely existent downtown.

But I knew this place. It had been one of many don't-blink-or-you'll-miss-it towns we'd hidden in when I was a child. And I knew just where to go. So he wouldn't freak out if he woke up and found us gone, I scratched out a note for Zac and left it on the bed.

"Come on," I whispered, taking Ashe by the hand. "Let's go for a walk."

WE SUPER-SPEEDED A MILE down the road to the town square and stopped in front of the Mueller County Library, built in 1867, as the sign out front boasted.

"When I said somewhere quiet..." Ashe said with a chuckle.

"What's quieter than a library? A closed one at that."

We walked around back where the Bookmobile was parked and approached the building, which had a back door with a set of concrete steps much like the one in the back of the prison. No silver, thankfully.

"How do you suppose we get in?" Ashe asked. "They'll have security alarms, won't they? Or a security guard?"

"Hmm, let's see if I can remember..." I walked behind some bushes that lined the wall. "Ah, yes, there it is." An egress window covered with a heavy iron grate yawned up at me from the mulched earth. I hadn't been strong enough at the time to open it, but my mother was. I bent and lifted the grate. The rusty hinges creaked, and I winced, hoping no one had heard it. I hopped down inside the egress, my boots slipping a little on the wet leaves and mud beneath.

Ashe looked down into the hole. "Locked?"

"Let's see." I didn't see any evidence of motion sensors, no heat signatures inside either. I tried the screen. It slid open fine. Then I tried the window. I couldn't be too rough, or I'd risk breaking the glass. It stuck a little, dousing my hopes at first, but then finally gave way and slid aside.

"Come on," I whispered.

Ashe hopped down beside me. I dropped down into the basement, and he followed.

It smelled just like I remembered – like old books, ink, wood, and musty earth. I stepped across the concrete floor. The only light came from the one left on in the stairwell. It was plenty enough to see the place had barely changed in the decade or so since I'd last slept here. Wood shelves held messy stacks of uncategorized books and magazines. Some of them were just too old to be handled, some were torn or damaged by water or fire, some were donations that had yet to find a home on the public shelves upstairs.

"Well, it's quiet," Ashe said.

"Very, except for him."

The misty form of a little boy appeared in front of us. Ashe jumped. "Holy shit!"

"Hey, Chip, how's it going?" I asked.

The ghostly face of a long-dead nine-year-old smiled back at me. His voice sounded far away, like someone whispering at the end of a long, echoing tunnel. "Wren, you're all grown up! I didn't think you'd come back."

"Neither did I. This is my friend Ashe." I did a double take at the tough vampire man frozen beside me. He was bone white, eyes wide as silver-dollar pancakes. "Oh, come on. You're a vampire. You're a lot scarier than he is."

"Never seen a ghost before, mister?" Chip asked, his misty head tilting to one side.

Ashe shook his head.

"Wow." I laughed. "You know, we're not that different. He's just without the benefit of a physical body."

"Yeah, it kind of stinks," Chip affirmed. "Playing ball is hard when you don't have hands anymore. But Wren taught me how to concentrate enough to roll a ball to her."

I smiled, remembering how we had become friends during those nights when my mother went out to work a temp job or hunt for food. We'd played and talked for hours.

"Oh, um...nice to meet you," Ashe said, relaxing a bit.

"Pleasure's all mine, sir," Chip answered, followed by a polite, misty bow.

"Chip died in a fire here back in 1907. He's pretty famous though. A lot of ghost-hunters have tried to find him."

"Those fellas are silly," Chip said, then added in a mocking voice, "*Is there anyone here? Can you make a sound for us? What's your name?* Sometimes I roll a ball or poke one of them just to watch them go bonkers. It's fun."

Ashe was smiling now instead of cringing. "I don't blame you for messing with them."

"I bet they'd wet their pants if they saw your vampire teeth."

I cleared my throat. "Say, Chip, my friend and I are kind of on a date. Could you go keep watch upstairs and give us some alone time?"

The ghost boy nodded, whooshing away from us with a disembodied giggle. His sing-song voice drifted up the stairs. "Wren and Ashe, sittin' in a tree, k-i-s-s-i-n-g."

"He's a sweet kid," Ashe said, pulling me into his arms. "Shame he's stuck here, though."

"He can cross over any time he wants, but he likes it here."

Ashe searched my eyes, appearing like he hadn't heard a word I'd just said. His hand drifted to my ass and squeezed. "Have you ever fucked in a library before?"

"I haven't. Let's do something about that." I led him into the unused brick-floored storage room at one end of the basement. It was dark and cobwebby, a relic from the original building.

"Uh, here? I mean, I'm game, but I think my queen deserves better."

"Watch." I ventured to an empty bookcase, hoping no one had found what I was looking for. The old, rusty metal shelves had a solid gray MDF board backing my mother had added. I slid one side of the bookcase out. Faint potpourri-scented, musty air whooshed out, and I led Ashe into the little hidden room. My eyes had a harder time adjusting here with the absence of outside light, but I found the oil lamp sitting on the table where we'd left it and the box of matches beside it.

I lifted off the glass globe, struck a match, and lit the wick. The fire blazed to life. I replaced the globe and lifted the lamp to look around at the little cozy place I'd called home for a few months. It had been my favorite place of all. I'd decorated the brick walls with pictures of movie stars and musicians I'd cut out from magazines. Images of Humphrey Bogart and Boris Karloff squared off with Jimi Hendrix and Gene Simmons above the fold-out sofa bed I'd shared with my mother.

"You are just full of surprises, aren't you?" Ashe said, stepping farther into the room. He looked around at the sheet-covered furniture, dusty books, and cassette radio that sat on a small wooden shelf.

My mother had left it like that, thinking we might return. Instead, she'd whisked me away one night, and we never came back.

I picked up a familiar book. "Mama read this to me a couple times. One of my favorite bedtime stories."

"Bram Stoker's *Dracula*?" Ashe said, one corner of his mouth curved into a half smile. "You know that's not a how-to manual, right?"

"I do now. For a long time, I thought if I concentrated hard enough, I could turn into a bat." The funny memory served as a reminder that my mother had left me virtually clueless about how to be a real vampire or that others like me existed. I sighed. Maybe coming here was a bad idea after all.

Ashe went to the radio and pressed the play button.

I thought the batteries would surely be dead, but instead, Janis Joplin's guitar scratched to life, the bluesy sound filling the small space with music. It charged the stale air and drove out the Debbie Downer mood threatening to ruin my night.

Ashe whipped off one of the furniture covers, revealing an old leather armchair. Then he whisked me into his arms and started dancing with me. Hand on my ass, he pulled me against him, against the hardness I couldn't wait to enjoy. We kissed, and my symbol throbbed, buzzing in a rhythm like a timer.

It *was* time. Time to make him mine for good.

"I need to be inside you," he whispered in my ear. Ashe pulled my shirt over my head, threw it aside. I did the same with his. Pants followed, then underwear. And then we were skin to skin, no barriers, no time to waste.

He picked me up; my legs wrapped around his waist. I could feel the tip of his dick teasing me, making me wet and ready, painfully so. My fangs emerged, and so did his. My eyes locked onto his copper ones that grew redder by the second. He lowered himself to sit on the chair, my knees holding me just a hair's breadth above his dick.

"Do you have any idea how gorgeous you are?" he said, but I put a finger to his lips.

I'd heard similar lines from a couple of guys I slept with who were drunk and didn't realize I was a vampire. I'd left before they woke and never looked back. But with Ashe, it actually sounded sincere, like something deeper than a one-night stand.

"Enough talking." I lowered myself in one smooth, quick movement, until he was seated deep inside me. The symbol on my arm shot lightning-hot streaks straight to my core.

Ashe snarled and made a growl that sounded more animal than man. He clamped his hands on my waist. I'd released something powerful, primal. There was no turning back now.

CHAPTER TWELVE

Ashe

Oh. Shiiiiit.

She was so wet, so tight, so perfect wrapped around my dick that I almost came inside her right then. So I lost myself in the distraction of her full lips and kissed her, hard, rough, almost like a punishment. She moaned as she matched my intensity, her tongue flicking and tasting, and she began to move on top of me, thrusting in time to our kiss. My skin couldn't get enough of hers, and my hands roamed everywhere, over her ass, up her rib cage to her perfect tits. All the while, the symbol on my arm shot wild hot streaks straight to my cock which. Wasn't. Helping.

I needed more of her. I needed to rut against her like a savage beast. I needed to fuck her brains out, soothe her back together, and then do it all over again.

"Wren..." It was a warning, or the start of one, but one look at her wet, kiss-swollen lips, her fevered eyes, her body writhing hard against mine, and that was it. Any control I might've had snapped.

"Wha— Oh!" Her mouth formed a perfect O as I stood us both up, still joined, our hips still thrusting, and dropped us to the fold-out bed which was covered with a sheet.

My hands went protectively behind her head when she almost hit the brick wall, but that was the beginning and end of gentle as I stretched out on top of her. Then I went balls deep inside of her again and again, and my mouth found hers. She met each of my thrusts with little cries and soft moans as she wound her fingers through the hair at the back of my head and held on.

"Ashe... Ashe!" She arched her long neck back, the cords pulling tight. Her slick inner walls pulsed and clamped down hard on my dick, just about ripping it off with the force of her orgasm. Which was fine. So, so much better than fine. But I couldn't hang on any longer.

I wanted to. I wanted to fuck her straight into next week, but the electric storm surging from my wrist centered all at once at the base of my cock.

Her copper eyes met mine, half open and sated, and she winked.

I came, hard, great waves rippling all the way down to my toes and back again, never-ending. My hips slapped against hers as I kept thrusting into her, and my orgasm lasted so long that she came again. We rode each other through it, eventually slowing, until we lay there grinning like idiots.

Our symbols glowed in matching rhythms like a heartbeat. Like synchronized heartbeats. Weird.

"*Damn*," she said, as she hugged me to her chest.

I laughed, feeling lightweight, relieved in every way possible, and almost already halfway asleep.

She blinked at her symbol and rubbed her thumb over it. "That was amazing."

"It was mostly me and my know-how, and not our symbols," I said, playing my fingers through her hair. "Just FYI."

She laughed, a throaty, pure sound that wrapped around me even tighter than her arms. "If you say so, big guy."

I nuzzled against her chest, my chin grazing the side of her tit, and everything about this felt right. Like we were made to fit together just like this while Wren reigned over the Southern Clan...with four other guys at her back.

Could I be willing to share her? Right now, no. Mostly because I was still inside her, but not just that. Sharing her with other guys would likely trigger some jealousy, even in me. Especially in me. It might even trigger some triggers. I had no right to feel like I owned Wren, though, especially when she had a greater role to play that was more important than the state of my heart. My heart would be fine, for the most part. Or fine-ish. Without her, the Southern Clan wouldn't be because Queen Ravana ruled without a heart. I'd known that even before she was framing me for murder. Allegedly, I supposed, since I had no proof.

"Your thoughts are louder than our sex was," she murmured against the top of my head. "Anything I should know?"

"I'm just thinking about you." I smoothed my hand over her shoulder, mesmerized by the silky feel and the shadows from the oil lamp flickering over it. "Thinking about what's going to happen."

"Me too."

"I don't want to hurt you, Wren."

"You didn't."

"No, I mean...good. But I meant on the inside. I hurt your feelings before at Edna's Itchen, and I can't do that again. Seeing that..." I shook my head at the memory of Jessica bruised and beaten, but that had been nothing compared to the hurt and betrayal in her eyes. Yes, it was weird to be thinking about my sister right then, but seeing her like that had destroyed me right down to my soul. It had hurt even more with Wren because *I'd* been the one who put it there. "Seeing people hurt like that... It's like my Achilles' heel."

"Well, now I know how to manipulate you without even really trying. Thanks for making it so easy." She pressed a kiss to my forehead and then ruffled my hair. "I'm kidding of course."

I laughed against her skin. "If you say so."

We stayed like that, with me still on top of her, and both of us drifted off to sleep. Sometime later, a horrible buzzing chime sounded like an alarm, and I sprang up off of Wren, so groggy that I had no idea what was happening or even where I was.

Oh yeah. The library. A normally quiet place. What was that sound? I lurched in the direction it came from while Wren groaned and rolled to her other side, hiking up a blanket around her bare shoulder. I had no idea how long I'd slept, so if it was daytime, people in the library could surely hear the noise.

I kicked through our discarded clothes, scanning the entire area, when my phone slid out of my pants pocket and onto the floor. The screen flashed white in time with the chime, indicating...something. I picked up the phone and looked at the screen. Jessica's number had texted me back multiple times in rapid fire, one for each of the annoying chimes.

Team Edward.

He's vampy.

He's rich.

He's hot.

He drives like a maniac but believes in seat belts.

I'm also on Team Jacob.

Why choose?

Where's my $5000?

I texted back: *Have you fed Edgar?*

There were only a handful of people who knew who her pet iguana Edgar was, and I happened to be one of them. She would figure out it was me she was texting. I figured if I got a text back, she wasn't trying to hide from me in shame. If she didn't text me back, well...I supposed that meant she didn't want to talk to the person she'd called the cops on. Or...something had happened to her, but it didn't.

The phone lay quiet in my palm as Wren slept like the dead beside me. I had to admit this stung a little, this long pause from Jessica. She might be dialing the police right now to have them track this number since it could have been her who'd sent them to her apartment to arrest me. I'd told her Devin was dead, after all. Didn't matter, at least the phone part. I'd chuck it in a dumpster soon enough.

But first, since I was up, might as well take care of some business. Like leaving instructions with Ben and Joe to shift ownership of Invite Us In Cleaners to them if they didn't hear back from me within a certain time-frame. I gave myself three days to clear my own name of two murders, and if I didn't, I would need to vanish for a very long time, hopefully with Wren. According to the news articles I looked up to gain some insight, even I could believe I was guilty.

I must've fallen asleep on the bed while reading about what a horrible person I was, because I woke to lips skimming up my jaw and a soft hand sliding over my chest. I sure hoped I knew this person. And I sure hoped her name was Wren.

I groaned low in my throat as I turned my head to face her, then smiled at how perfect she looked lying next to me. She reached up to touch my jaw and grazed her lips over mine, her yellow eyes dancing with firelight and heavy with lust. Her hips drove into my side once, twice, dry-humping me from underneath her blanket while she ran her tongue underneath my bottom lip.

My dick, already hard, hardened even more and throbbed to be inside her. "Good morning to you too," I said and wrapped her up closer so she could feel exactly what she did to me.

"Guess who I dreamed about?" she purred.

"Gene Simmons?" I pointed above the bed to his poster.

"You guessed it." She pushed me flat on my back, freed herself from her blanket, and straddled me, her wetness pressed right up against my pulsing balls. Then she began to grind against me and leaned down, trailing slow kisses up my chest. "God, you're good."

"Damn right."

I wasn't even inside her yet, but I was *this* close to coming. Yet just like before, I wanted all of her at once.

She arched her back, which thrust her ass into the air, and I grabbed it and squeezed. My other hand went to the back of her head and fisted in her hair until she found my mouth with hers. Our tongues battled at the same tempo as our bucking hips. I slipped my hand from her ass and slid it down her smooth stomach, and then down farther to feel just how wet she was. We both groaned when I pushed two fingers up inside her.

"You're fucking drenched, Wren."

Her hips began to go wild, pressing her harder into the palm of my hand, but I quickly replaced my fingers with my cock because I was sure she was about to come. I slid my dick home, feeling her tighten around me, feeling how slippery and amazing she was, and she kept up the same pace as she had on my fingers.

She arched her back and sat up, which rocked her tits forward into my hands. I fondled them, leaned up to suck and bite them, and then she came with a violent shudder. She cried out as she squeezed around me, but I silenced her with a hard kiss. Her pulsing wetness, and the heated sparks from my wrist symbol, pulled an orgasm from the base of my spine and unwound it fast, straight into her. We swallowed each other's groans, held tight, and then sagged against each other when the last of the aftershocks faded.

With a small laugh, she laid her head on my shoulder. "If your goal is to change the way I walk, I have a feeling it's mission accomplished."

I chuckled into her hair and then breathed her in, her sex smell, the clean soapy scent of her skin, the sexy rose smell of her hair. I couldn't believe I was lucky enough to touch her. I had to admit, it made me want to pound my chest a little, but also hold her close.

"What's that sound?" she asked.

When I let my mind drift away from her, I heard it too. Similar to the sound my phone had made before but slightly less annoying.

"I think my phone might be ringing." Maybe it was my landlord who was calling to say he did have backup tapes proving someone had forced their way into my apartment to plant evidence. Or maybe it was Jessica.

"Oh." Wren, still joined with me, reached over to get it from where I must've dropped it on the floor and then pressed a button. Her yellow eyes stuck on the screen, and then she froze. "Ashe."

The phone still rang, and I held out my hand for it. "Let me answer, and then I need to get rid of this phone."

She jerked the phone from my seeking fingers and climbed off of me quickly as if she couldn't wait to get away. Her gaze was laser-focused on the phone, but then she finally flicked it up to me—sharp, lethal, fucking pissed. "When were you going to tell me you helped murder my mother?"

CHAPTER THIRTEEN

WREN

WHOEVER HAD BEEN CALLING had given up and left a text.
Explain.

A picture followed. It was somewhat fuzzy, a photo of a news broadcast taken with a cell phone camera. The call letters in the bottom corner read VTV. The still footage showed uniformed guards like those in the prison, holding up a silver net, darkened with old, dried blood. The news snippet below: *Escaped prisoner Ashe Jensen being sought in connection with Queen Bronwen's murder and the murder of Devin Newport, one of her mates. Suspect considered armed and dangerous. Last seen with unknown human male and female vampire.*

The image of the net's tarnished mesh burrowed straight into the memories I'd tried to entomb in the recesses of my mind. Her screams still echoed in my ears. The image of her panicked eyes was something I'd never unsee. I was hidden in a dumpster, peeking from a tiny space beneath the lid. She projected her last words into my head—something she'd never done before.

Stay hidden no matter what. I love you, Princess.

Seconds later, a knife blade flashed. It tore through flesh and sawed into bone. Gurgling, thrashing, and blood followed. So much blood... The only thing I could do was to sink down onto the rotting refuse, hugging my knees, my fist pressed hard against my mouth to stifle a scream.

I thought they might find me, but they didn't. They must not have known I existed, which was probably why she had told me to hide rather than run from her attackers. I shuffled through my memories, painful as they were, to remember if Ashe's face had been among her killers. But it had taken several men to restrain her. I didn't get a good look at all their faces.

Even so, I had eventually managed to kill most of them. *Most*, except for a few stragglers and a man I'd all but given my heart to already.

Ashe sat silent, staring at me with wide, unblinking eyes, his face turning paler by the second. "I can explain."

"Is this why you were in prison?" I tossed the phone to him, giving him a moment to see the news blurb someone had texted him.

His face paled. His gaze flicked toward mine, and his voice sounded shaky and hollow. "I didn't kill your mother."

"How old were you back then?" My mother had been nearly a hundred years old, thanks to slow-burning vampire genetics. Ashe could very well be her age or older.

He focused on the floor as though counting it up, then lifted his gaze to me again. "I was fifteen."

"Old enough to kill, then."

"No, I'm telling you, someone framed me for this. I haven't killed anyone, I swear."

I dressed in a blinding two milliseconds, my skin still tingling and sensitive from being entwined with his. Everything about it had felt so right, but then what did I know about right when it came to vampires? Nothing. Zilch. A big fat zero except what I'd learned over the course of a few days. And I couldn't even trust all that to be true. Not with the net that helped end my mother's life connected to the name of someone destined to be my mate.

Ashe dressed in a blur as well and was beside me before I could figure out what to do next. "Wren, please. You have to listen."

He put a hand on my shoulder, but I pushed him...okay, more like threw him against the wall. He braced himself with his arms so his head didn't smash into the bricks. I thought for a moment he might retaliate, but the flash of anger in his eyes soon chilled into fear and uncertainty.

"I don't *have* to do anything." It would probably have been easier to just kill him than trying to decide if he was innocent or guilty. I could have gone on the run again, grabbed Birdie and took off to parts unknown. I knew how to disappear. What the fuck did I know about being a queen anyway?

He reached for me again, but I stepped back.

"Don't touch me. They don't just put people into prison for nothing. Why would anyone frame you for murder?"

"I don't know." He averted his eyes then swallowed hard.

I shoved him up against the wall again, my hand flat against his chest, pinning him there. "You know something. Talk."

He stiffened but kept his hands to his sides. "The night I was arrested, I...had plans to kill someone."

"Who? Me?"

"No!" He looked genuinely wounded, but was it just good acting? "It was a vampire named Devin. He beat the shit out of my sister six years ago. I warned him if he came near her again, I'd kill him. I saw a picture of them together just a few days ago and decided to keep my word. But when I got to the hotel, he was already dead. I have no idea who killed him or why, but I was arrested not long after. They said I was also locked up because someone found that net in my apartment. I've never owned anything like that. Someone wanted to pin your mother's death on me. I never even met her, Wren. I swear. I don't know how this is all connected yet."

"Pardon me if I'm having a hard time believing you."

He raked his fingers through his blond hair and pulled so it spiked up. "Maybe they were trying to flush you out. Maybe they knew I was your mate or that Zac was looking for us. Maybe Zac's involved. Hell if I know. All I know is that we belong together. Whatever this connection is, it's real. I don't think I could lie to you even if I tried."

"I need to be alone for a while." Tears pricked the corners of my eyes. I hadn't cried since the night my mother, an apparent queen, had been taken from me. I wasn't about to start now.

I started out of the hidden room, but Ashe zipped in front of me.

"Don't. Please. It's not safe out there."

My fangs emerged. I leveled a death glare at him, my voice rumbling with an all-too-predatory growl. "Not for you, maybe. Step aside."

He hesitated, lips twitching as though he wanted to protest. But thankfully, his desire to survive won over the stubbornness. He stepped aside, head lowered in reverence for his queen, I guessed. Whatever. I couldn't put blind faith into him just because we'd fucked. But something in me told me he was being truthful. How much could I trust that instinct?

I started toward the stairs, but a stubborn pebble of guilt irritated my conscience. "I won't go far. Stay here."

I zipped upstairs onto the library's main floor, where Chip's misty form hovered over a wooden train set meant to distract living kids so their parents could read in peace. He had to concentrate hard in order to pick up anything. I must have broken his concentration. The caboose he held fell through his hand and knocked a few train cars off the tracks. I glanced up at the security camera aimed in his direction and smiled. The library staff would be in a tizzy tomorrow when they viewed the footage of trains being tossed about. That in turn would bring on a slew of ghost hunters for Chip to mess with.

Chip floated over to me. "Where's your friend?"

We spoke in almost silent whispers only ghosts and vampires, not security cameras or humans, could pick up.

"He's asleep," I lied and really hoped the little spirit hadn't spied on us. Even a dead boy didn't need to see our mating frenzy.

"Okay. It's been really quiet up here. Want to play?"

"Sure. For a minute. Hide-and-seek?"

His mouth stretched into a ghostly grin. "You're it!" He whooshed into the stacks, disappearing with a poof of white mist left behind.

Covering my eyes, I counted out loud to ten. "Ready or not, here I come!" All I had to do was use my night vision to pick up his cold temperature signature. But he was good at hiding inside solid objects to conceal his cold energy. "Hey, no hiding in the walls or floor, remember?"

His hollow laughter bounced around the room, so I couldn't pinpoint his location by sound. "Okay, but you can't use your superpower eyes either."

"As you wish." I closed my eyes, depending on scent and sound to guide my footsteps. I knew every squeak in the floorboards, but a few things had been moved around since I'd last roamed the building. I banged my shin into a new chair in the expanded children's area and bit my lip so I didn't yell out a bad word that the cameras and Chip didn't need to hear.

Chip giggled. Closer this time. I made my way to the big plastic playhouse at the rear corner of the room by big windows that I imagined let in tons of warm sunlight for all the kids who enjoyed the space. The air around me cooled. Smiling, I realized what was "warm" or "hot" for human hide-and-seek is the opposite when you play with ghosts. I could also smell lingering smoke that carried a faint whiff of charred flesh. Poor kid. At least he'd died from the smoke before the fire burned him beyond recognition.

I ducked down at the playhouse door and opened my eyes. "Gotcha!"

"Aw, man! I forgot how good you are at hide-and-seek."

"Want me to hold my nose too?"

Chip laughed. "Nah. Your turn to hide."

He covered his eyes with his cold, misty hands, the transparency of which probably didn't block much of his sight. It didn't matter. Playing with Chip brought back the good times I'd had as a kid and helped settle the battle of whether to trust Ashe that was going on in my head. I zipped past the reference shelves and graphic novels, straight up the spiral steel staircase that led to the meeting room. It rattled a little, which would probably give me away. Oh well, at least I was having fun.

I decided to hide just outside on the fire escape. I unlocked the window, quietly slid it up and hopped out, leaving it cracked open.

Chip's voice echoed from downstairs. "Ready or not, here I come!"

He'd find me in no time, but I squatted down below the window sill. I wanted some fresh air to cool the heat Ashe had left behind with his lips, hands, and other pleasurable parts. Being this close to him pulled at my desire like a rubber band about to snap. Maybe distance was a bad thing? Would we both disintegrate if we got too far apart? Yet another critical piece of information that would have come in handy before I fucked him and sealed our bond.

What was I supposed to do if I ended up with all five of them bonded to me? Would I ever get a moment's peace? For a girl who'd been on her own for most of her life, suddenly being glued to five other people was about as appealing as pulling out a fang with rusty pliers.

While ruminating over things I had no clue about, Chip materialized on the fire escape, touching my face with his ice-cold fingers.

"Hey, you cheated, ghost boy."

"No, I didn't. You said don't go through walls or floors. I went through the window instead." He grinned, showing spaces where he'd lost a couple teeth as a mortal kid. I guess they don't grow in after you're dead.

"Well, you got me there."

"My turn to hide?"

"Sorry, little man, I better go check on Ashe and get out of here before the place opens." I stood, reaching for the window to go back inside.

But then I caught a whiff of something. It was a nasty scent, like rotten garlic, something my prey often used to hide their smell...

A hard object poked my back. "Chip, what are you—?"

Searing pain choked the rest of my words into a long, low wail. Fiery currents rippled along my spine into my head, arms, and legs. My surroundings wobbled like an earthquake had hit. I lost my balance, stumbled into the fire escape railing, and over I went.

Chip's cold ethereal hands tried to grab me as I fell, but he couldn't hold on. I hit the sidewalk flat on my back. I couldn't tell up from down. Vertigo scrambled all sense of direction. A blurry head with some kind of weird hat loomed over me.

"Well, what do we have here? A wannabe queen? I know somebody who'll pay me good for you." His voice was deep, hoarse, and distant like someone talking on a tin can phone.

Next thing I knew, hard fingers clamped around my ankles. My body slid across rough pavement that felt as unsteady as a rocking boat.

I heard Chip's voice, louder than ever before, calling, "Ashe! Hurry! Wren needs help!"

Before everything faded to nothing, I smiled through the delirium. Those paranormal teams would have one hell of an EVP to fawn over.

CHAPTER FOURTEEN

ASHE

I LET WREN GO out of the hidden room even though the urge to go after her, to beg her to believe me, burned deep. This wasn't how I wanted her to find out. I wanted to have proof I hadn't done it first, and right now, I only had my word. Not much at all for an escaped fugitive with two murders he didn't commit hanging over his head like two sharp blades. With how things had been going lately, they'd come crashing down any second with no warning.

I couldn't blame Wren for thinking I'd killed her mother after seeing the planted evidence against me in a video text from my sister. Jessica had texted back with: *Explain.*

I really, really wished I could.

Can we meet somewhere? I texted back, my fingers shaking a little. It meant a lot that Jessica still had enough faith in me to want me to explain. But she still had quite a bit of explaining to do herself, like that picture of her and Devin with a date stamp of only a week ago, that picture of her with shorter hair than she had now. Even vampire hair didn't grow that fast. Which meant that picture hadn't been taken a week ago.

Hogwarts. 5x5.

I nodded, even though she obviously couldn't see me. I knew what she was talking about. In the backyard of our parents' old house, a garden shed with turrets stood near the back, a fantastical mystery compared to everything else in Brightwell. It had reeled Jessica in right when we'd moved there with its imaginary promise of vicious battles between good and evil. She'd always been such a dreamer. If I ever wondered where she was—and I could probably count on one hand all the times I had wondered back then—she was most likely galloping around the garden shed with her broom.

She wanted to meet there at 5x5 or 2500 hours in military time. Yes, yes, military time only had twenty-four hours, unless you were our dad, an uptight Southern Clan Navy veteran, who despised procrastination and "lazing about."

You have the same twenty-five hours in a day as everyone else, he'd tell us. *Use that time wisely.*

Mom, the more chill of the two, decided that extra hour was between midnight and one. Then she'd sneak a sip of wine straight from the bottle when she thought no one was looking.

Ok. Delete this message, I texted.

She sent me a thumbs-up, the most passive aggressive emoji ever.

Meeting her at Hogwarts meant we'd need to go back to Brightwell tomorrow night, something I wasn't too keen on, but I couldn't just leave her without saying goodbye. And I had a feeling I *was* leaving, permanently, because this thing with Wren and helping her take the crown wouldn't just go away, whether she hated my guts or not.

The symbol on my wrist went ice cold. I gasped and stared down at it.

"Ashe! Hurry! Wren needs help!"

My blood went arctic at the panic in Chip's voice that echoed from upstairs. My muscles froze to my veins. I threw the door of the hidden room open and stumbled out, terror stiffening my spine as I raced up the stairs three steps at a time.

"Where?" I shouted, scouring the dark library.

"Up here!"

His misty form waved from an upper level accessible from a metal spiraling staircase. I zipped up there, shaking the structure so much, I thought it might collapse. Chip hovered on the other side of the upper level by the fire escape door, his ghostly hand waving frantically.

I sprinted toward him at full speed, knocking into book stands and spilling the shiny new books to the floor. One of them skidded right under my next footfall, and when the sole of my shoe touched it, my leg skated out from underneath me. I crashed onto the thin brown carpet, hip first, then shoulder and head, which bounced. Twice. Pain flared, but I ignored it and untangled my limbs with a snarl before I stood.

A female vampire with poofy dark hair smiled up at me from the cover of the book that had taken me down. A self-help book titled *How to Grow Your IQ by Drinking Smart People*.

Oh, the irony.

I dragged myself up when three things happened at once. What sounded like a door slammed just outside where Chip was madly waving me. The lights flipped on. And my cell started blaring its ring.

I hauled balls out of there and tore through the fire escape window. An ear-shattering alarm cut through the library. If whoever turned on the lights didn't know someone was here before, they sure as hell would now.

Not my concern. Neither was my ringing cell at the moment.

The fire escape opened into an alley that reeked of sweaty garbage and pee. Two large blue dumpsters sat against the opposite brick wall on either side of a closed metal door. About ten feet to the left near the alley entrance sat a parked black van that might as well have had *Free Candy* scrawled along the sides. The few windows it had were painted black.

"Chip?" I hissed into the alley, at a complete loss of how ghosts actually worked. Could he hear me through the library walls? "Where is she?"

I hurtled off the fire escape balcony toward the metal door opposite me. Locked. When I turned, Chip's bluish form appeared in the open window of the fire escape above me. He pointed toward the van, but then his eyes widened.

"Ashe! Behind you!"

I didn't even have a chance to look. Something hard rammed into my back. Pain fired to all points of my body hard enough to bring tears to my eyes. The black van swam behind them, so close but seeming to grow farther away.

No. They couldn't take Wren from me, but my muscles weren't cooperating to do much about it. I seemed to be folding in on myself, crumpling to the pockmarked alley filled with puddles I sure hoped were just rainwater.

"Well, this is sure something," a male voice said from behind me. Familiar, especially his zero-fucks-given tone. When he circled around me, his dusty leather fedora confirmed it, as did the arrogant twist of his mouth he always wore.

He was the vampire I'd hired to keep tabs on Jessica and make sure she never saw Devin again. The vampire who'd sent me the photo of Jessica and Devin together with the date stamp of a week ago, which now appeared to be inaccurate, at least according to Jessica. This couldn't be a coincidence that he was here, now, reducing me to uselessness with a stun gun while he stole Wren away.

"Charles Fucking Ford," I spat through clenched teeth, fighting to control the spasms still rioting through me.

His alligator boots came to a stop inches from my head, the same murky green color as the band around his fedora. He wore tan pants and a brick-red, button-up shirt rolled up his forearms. An expert no-questions-asked freelancer/lady-killer, so I'd heard, but I hoped with all my might that last part was figurative.

Over his head and to the left, Chip appeared in the window of the library and began to frantically unscrew the fire escape from the brick wall, his ghostly face scrunched in concentration. I could guess what the little ghost had planned. Impressive, especially if it worked.

Best to keep Charles's attention on me so he wouldn't see it coming.

After hitching up his thick leather belt with two holsters stuffed with a stun gun and a real gun, Charles squatted down in front of me. "I know, I know. Dick move, huh? It turns out there are always people who can pay better, and those people become my new best friends. Much better than my old best friends."

"The picture," I ground out.

"Was a fake. Taken from years ago and then doctored with last weeks' date. So easy, I did it while in between some girl's legs. Someone really wanted to drag you into the spotlight and see what you would do to Devin, and they paid better than you did."

"Queen Ravana hired you."

"You're not as stupid as you look. She offered quite a pretty penny for you." He clapped me on the shoulder, hard enough to revive the fading electrical pulses to near-screaming. "So sorry that it came to this."

I groaned, the loose gravel knifing into the side of my face while my body shuddered. "Let her go and take me instead."

He gave a humorless laugh. "No can do. Not to mention your girl is a dead ringer for former Queen Bronwen. I'm sure Queen Ravana will be just as curious as I am about that."

I bared my teeth and fought to get my arms underneath me to pull myself up enough to chomp out his eyeballs and spit them down his throat. But I only managed to burrow myself deeper into the gravel. I'd have to keep talking to distract him. "The queen will kill her."

"That's the thing about mercenaries. We don't have morals or"—he shuddered—"feelings."

I glanced up, and then grinned. "You're about to feel something."

With a long groan, the fire escape platform broke free from the wall and plummeted on a direct path towards Charles's head. He whirled then hurtled out of the way just in time and fell back on his ass, his hand keeping his fedora on his head as he went.

Part of the platform had caught at an angle on the opposite building's wall, and the ladder hung free like a pendulum, back and forth, creaking like a rusty swing.

I ticked my gaze up to Chip in the window, but he was nowhere in sight. Hopefully he had more up his ghostly sleeves.

"What the hell was that?" Charles demanded from a few feet away, his gaze on the swinging ladder between us.

"Give me back the girl," I growled.

"Look, I already explained to you my methods." Charles hauled himself to his feet and started toward me, keeping an eye on the ladder so it wouldn't hit him. "I go where the money is, and for this size of paycheck, I'm taking you *and* the girl with me."

The ladder stilled right in front of him, pulling him up short, but it didn't seem to be because of Chip. He'd vanished.

Silence stretched over the alley, as well as a bone-deep chill. A sudden wind picked up the trash on the ground and skipped it over the wet gravel toward Charles.

He looked up.

Something monstrous clambered down the ladder with a loud roar straight for him. Something Chip-shaped, but also not. Nightmare-fuel with dead black eyes and three-feet-long fangs in the same pattern as Chip's missing teeth. He hurtled toward Charles's upturned face and wide eyes, and then shot right into him. Charles's mouth hung open as his face took on the same bluish hue as Chip. His eyes widened even more, and he let out a weird squawk. Then all color completely leached from his face as Chip reappeared behind Charles with the same loud roar.

Chip surged *through* Charles, turning him even bluer, which seemed to freeze Charles to the ground. He held completely still while Chip vanished into the air.

Now was my chance to get up and get to Wren. I needed to get *up*. But I couldn't. I had no control over my body.

Charles began to move then, slowly, and then as if he'd stepped out of an iceberg, he shook it off. Looking even more dead than normal, Charles staggered toward his van without a backward glance, dove behind the wheel, cranked the engine, and then peeled out of there.

Taking Wren with him to the queen who would definitely kill her once she realized Wren was far from dead.

Helplessness just about swallowed me whole. I wanted to scream, chase after them, anything more than what I was currently doing.

Chip appeared in front of me back in his little boy form, one hand on the ladder, his shoulders slumped and shaking. "I thought that bad man was just playing with us at first. This is all my fault."

"I'll get her back," I growled, and it was more of a vow to myself than to him.

With one clumsy, painful finger wiggle at a time, I finally dragged my phone from my pocket and immediately dropped half of it into the puddle next to my nose. Cursing, I flipped it out, spraying my mouth with whatever liquid it happened to be. Never mind the gross factor. The five-second rule had to apply to phones in questionable water too. It really, really had to.

With a combination of my nose and fingers, I dialed Zac at the hotel and about lost consciousness at the flood of relief when it connected.

"What happened?" Zac answered.

"He took Wren." It hurt to say it, because that made it true. But it also focused my mind on something other than the pain in my body as I forced myself into a sitting position.

"Fuck, Ashe. *Who* took Wren?"

Eventually, I stood on my own two feet, glaring after the van. "A dead man."

CHAPTER FIFTEEN

WREN

I OPENED MY EYES to darkness and cigar smoke but finally gathered enough streetlight through the windshield to see a silhouette of a man in the driver's seat of whatever van he'd used to kidnap me. He was driving like a crazy person, taking every turn on what seemed like two wheels. My head bounced around on the bare metal floor of the van. Apparently, my life had devolved into being tossed around in vehicles with bad drivers in my quest to be queen of the south or whatever.

I tried to sit up or roll over but couldn't. At first, I thought I was tied down, but my legs and arms, even my fingers and toes, wouldn't cooperate with my nervous system. I couldn't feel much of anything from the neck down.

Fuck my undead life.

It didn't seem to be daylight yet, so either I hadn't been out for long or we'd been driving a really long time. Homing in on the craptastic driver, I could only see a cool blue heat signature. Not human. Lovely. Yet another vampire who'd crawled out of the woodwork to complicate shit.

His eyes flicked upward, their reflection in the rearview mirror meeting mine. "Well now, looks like somebody's awake."

The strong southern drawl reminded me of a dollar-hungry televangelist. "Where'd you get that accent? Dumbfuck, Georgia?"

"Try South Carolina."

"No difference."

He chuckled, a deep rumbling sound that wasn't terrible.

"Who are you?" I asked.

"You first."

"Since you obviously have the upper hand, with me lying here limp as a withered dick, how about you throw me a bone? It would be mighty kind of you, sir," I added in my best Scarlett O'Hara voice.

"All right, then. I'm Charles. And you are?"

"Melody Songsmith."

"I call bullshit on that one. And we're here."

"Where's here, Charlie?"

"*Don't* call me Charlie," he spat.

What was up with that?

"Don't you worry your pretty imposter head now, darlin'. You won't be here long." Charles Don't Call Me Charlie resumed his charming southern drawl.

My eye twitched. Darlin'? As soon as I could get my limbs working again, I'd show him how much of a darlin' I could be.

"How about you don't call me darlin', and I won't call you Charlie. Deal?"

He shrugged. The van came to a stop. The soon to be a headless Charles got out. A few seconds later, he opened the rear doors of the van and dragged me out feet first. Thankfully, he didn't let my head smash onto the concrete. Instead, he eased it down gently, then dragged me none-too-gently through a fine layer of sawdust across the floor of what looked to be a woodshop. Extension cords hung from the rafters, swinging in the breeze like vipers waiting for their chance to strike.

My head bumped across a threshold and onto the scratchy AstroTurf of a smaller room. Charles dropped my feet, which landed with a numb thud, and opened a squeaky door to a cage as tall as a man and about twice as wide. I still couldn't see him clearly, except for an Indiana Jones kind of hat and a cigar dangling from his mouth.

"Seriously? A cage? I won't make a good pet."

"You're not a pet. You're a paycheck."

"You running some kind of vampire sex trafficking ring?"

"Nope." Charles scooped me up, tossed me over his shoulder like a bag of kitty litter, and walked into the cage. As he shifted my weight to put me down, I bared my fangs and bit down into his shoulder.

His cigar fell from his mouth as he cried out and tore me away, dropping me onto a musty-smelling mattress. "Damn it, you ruined my trench coat."

I spit out the shredded piece of said coat. The tough leather had only allowed my teeth to graze his skin. Traces of his blood lingered on my fangs. I licked it off, the taste of which was immediately intoxicating, like the best fucking wine I'd ever had. Were all vampires this yummy? Then I recalled the vampires I'd killed in the jail and Edna's Itchen.

No, they were pretty damn gross, come to think of it.

He bent to pick up his cigar, the end of which was now bent and smoldering. He started to stick it in his mouth, then growled and dropped it, squishing it under his boot. Thanks to the filtered security light coming in from the dirty windows in the overhead door, I got a better look at him. He had wide-set dark eyes, a confidently solid nose, and a chin dimple that wasn't nearly as impressive as Zac's but still worth a good lick or two.

But as he towered over me and my limp-as-a-wet-dishrag body, a touch of fear prickled the hairs on the back of my neck. It had been a very long time since I had been this vulnerable. In fact, I'd never been quite *this* vulnerable before. I wasn't a maiden-in-distress kind of girl, but I kept watching the still-open overhead door and listening in hopes that Zac or Ashe would come storming in and waste this guy's ass.

I willed my voice to be steady and converted my fear to the sharp tone of anger. "If you're planning on raping me, you better damn well kill me."

Charles grinned. "You think I'd stoop that low?"

"I may be wrong, but a man who paralyzes a woman and takes her to a remote building then tosses her onto a nasty mattress kind of screams sex offender."

Charles waved a hand at me, rolling his eyes before he ducked slightly and stepped out of the cage. He closed the door and turned a key in the lock. After closing the overhead door, he dragged a metal chair across the concrete floor. The legs screeched a high-pitched wail that could deafen a dead man. I gritted my teeth and turned my head as far away as I could, which wasn't very damn far, thanks to the numb rest of me.

Finally, the eardrum gouging stopped when he straddled the chair backwards, his elbows draped across the chair back. Removing his gloves, he drawled at me, "A little bird told me you're trying to impersonate a queen. Want to tell me about that...Wren?"

"Not particularly." Lovely. He knew my name. Our little rebel trio must've been making waves in the vampire community. That could be bad. Why had I ever agreed to this madness?

He pulled another cigar from his coat, then tossed his hat onto a nearby workbench. His messy chestnut-brown hair hung in his eyes before he shook it back. After striking a match on his boot, he lit the cigar and puffed, then let the smoke roll from his mouth.

"Those will kill you, you know," I added, wishing him dead, but in vain.

"Funny."

His chuckle triggered a flutter in my fingers. *My fingers!* Whatever he'd injected was starting to wear off. I had to lie still, though, until it wore off enough for me to bust out of here. The cage was fully boxed in, and from the looks of it, bolted onto the floor.

"I figure we have less than an hour until the Fangaway wears off and less than that before your buyers arrive. You might want to practice your bullshit story on me before they get here. They're not nearly as tolerant of lies as I am."

I squeezed my eyes shut and laughed, shaking my head before I looked straight at him. "Fangaway? What the fuck is that? Sounds like a dentist anesthetic."

The smirk he'd been wearing slid into a frown, and he looked away. "It worked, didn't it?"

"You really drugged me with a dentist anesthetic? What did you do, steal it when they were getting your Ninja Turtles toothbrush?" I laughed again, rolling my head to stare at the ceiling, my eyes searching for good hand and foot holds, and if I were lucky, a skylight. I couldn't fly, but I could jump like a jack rabbit and climb like a spider monkey. But no dice. Solid sheet-metal roof.

He hung his head, knocked some ashes from the cigar. "It was a Batman toothbrush," he mumbled. When he looked up, he wore a lopsided grin that did nice things to his face.

And then he went and ruined it with a hateful scowl again.

"You're stalling," he said. "I'll ask again, who are you? Because you look a whole lot like somebody that ought to be dead."

"Do I? And who would that be?"

"You tell me. All I know is that there's a big ol' bounty on your head, and the ones offering it are not nearly so merciful as I am."

"So Ravana's caught wind of me already?"

"Damn right. And what I'd really like to know is, why are you impersonating her dead sister?"

My legs and arms began to tingle. I could move a few toes within the privacy of my boots. "I'm not impersonating anyone."

"You're not fooling anyone. The old queen and her... They're dead." He shook one of his arms as though shaking off a fly, then rubbed it through his coat. "You look a hell of a lot like a dead queen. So why are you with a human guard dog and the vampire accused of that queen's murder?"

I'd have to choose my words carefully. Just how much did this guy know? Probably more than I did. I still didn't know if I could trust Zac or Ashe or anyone for that matter. But the good thing was I could finally feel the damp mattress under my hands.

Ignoring the gross factor, I kept still, but sensation was returning quickly all along my body. "Would it help if I told you that I had no idea she was a queen until yesterday?"

"Who do you mean? Ravana?"

"No. Bronwen."

"So, you *did* know her."

"I did."

"Did you kill her?"

The mere accusation sent a fiery heat into my fingers, which I curled into fists to keep from breaking through the cage. I still had a bit of unparalyzing left to do. Until then, I had to weigh the risks of honesty over lies. On one hand, if I convinced him I was Bronwen's daughter, he might drug me again so he could turn me over to Ravana quicker. Then again, if Zac and Ashe managed to get here in time to break me out, that knowledge could leave Ravana quaking in her heels. I decided to take the risk.

"Would *you* kill your own mother?" I asked.

His smirk slid away for a moment into open-mouthed shock. Then he huffed a laugh. "Nice try. Bronwen's daughter died along with her."

"Unless I had a sister I didn't know about, I'm afraid you are mistaken, sir."

"No." Charles's eyes turned blood red. He pointed his finger like a knife at me, then abruptly stood and stuck the cigar in his mouth before he commenced pacing like a caged animal. Funny, considering I was the one in the cage, just lying there chilling out. Well, not exactly, but you get my drift.

"Think about it. I look just like her. I mean, I'm good with disguises, but I'm not *that* good. This is no rubber mask. No wig or contacts, either. But I'm sure you already saw that for yourself."

That last thought made me shiver. He could have done anything to me when I was out cold. But my clothes were still intact, my lady bits still pleasantly sore from my time with Ashe. In fact, they ached again like they had when I'd first met Ashe, as if he were near.

"Come closer. Look again if you don't believe me. It's not like I can do much about it." Actually, I could feel everything now, and it was all I could do to lie still, especially when the symbols on my arm buzzed and burned in a fast rhythm. Ashe must be closing in.

The old 60s song rang out in my head, "My Boyfriend's Back"... And little Charlie Charles was gonna be in trouble.

Charles turned toward me, shook his arm again like it had fallen asleep, and rubbed it through his coat again. Had he accidentally injected himself? Or had I bitten him in my drugged stupor? Would serve him right either way.

He slowly approached the cage, squatted down about a foot from the bars. I looked right at him, batting my eyelashes and smiling with slightly puckered lips. It might have come off a little too much like Zoolander, but whatever.

His eyes roamed all over my face, likely checking for makeup lines, seams, a nylon skull cap. Things I kept tucked away in Birdie's trunk until I needed them. This close, I got a good look at his eyes. They were pretty for a kidnapper—a warm amber with flecks of dark brown. The frown he wore deepened the longer he looked. My arm (and lady bits) throbbed painfully. Ashe had to be very close.

Now was my chance, while Mr. Pretty-Eyed Kidnapper was caught like a fly in the web of my mesmerizing gaze. I sprang up and grabbed the bars. I'd rip this cage up like a tin can and stab Charles with a twisted shard of metal.

But instead, searing heat scorched my palms. The smell of burned skin invaded my nose. My fangs dropped involuntarily. I screamed and fell back onto the mattress, holding my shaking hands in front of me, and stared at my blistered and charred skin. It was worse than the sunburn I'd gotten when breaking Ashe out of jail. And hurt like a sumbitch times ten.

Charles had already leapt back, standing there with the chair held toward me, legs first, like he was fending off a circus lion. He was afraid. That was one thing I had going for me.

"Silver?" I groaned.

"Of course. I'm not *that* stupid. Electrified too...for her pleasure."

The metal had been so tarnished, I hadn't realized what it was. He approached again slowly and crouched down by the cage. His voice softened, as did his face. He looked almost regretful.

"If you're really Bronwen's daughter, answer this question. What was her middle name?"

"She didn't have one. At least that's what she told me."

His eyes narrowed a bit. "Lucky guess. Okay, then, here's another. Where did she always want to go on vacation?"

"What is this? Bank security questions?" At his insistent glare, I shrugged. "Fine. Disney World."

That time, his eyes went wide for a moment before they narrowed into his *I am skeptical vampire* frown. "Lots of people, and vampires, want to go there. I mean, we *could* go when the sun goes down, but who wants to spend all that money for a couple hours' worth of cheesy?"

"For hell's sake. Are we done here?" I realized then that I could grab the mattress and use it as a kind of battering ram to break through the bars. Sometimes, I could just kick myself. Silly Wren.

"No. One more. There was an old song she used to sing when she was scared as a little girl. What was it?"

"How would *you* know that?"

"Just answer the question."

Sighing, I closed my eyes and smiled, transported back to the day we had to sleep in a mausoleum in the middle of January. I remembered racing across the graveyard just before sunrise, her picking me up because I was too tired and cold to run anymore. We were relatively immune to cold, but that kind of cold threatened to freeze us solid. We huddled together in the dark cavern filled with long-dead corpses, wrapped in a tarp she had ripped from over a freshly dug grave. I shivered so much, I thought my fangs would break. She said we were playing "Race the Sun" to see how close we could get to sunrise before having to hide away again. Now I know her enemies must have been closing in or she wouldn't have risked us getting torched by the sun. The next night, she was killed. But for that one morning, wrapped in my mother's arms, I felt safe and loved, and had fallen asleep to the sound of her softly singing.

Eyes still closed, I said, "She didn't just sing it when she was a little girl. She sang it to *me*, too." I swallowed hard, allowing the lyrics to surface from where I'd buried them in my subconscious. Then I sang, *"The time has come, to be brave, to be who you're meant to be. The day is done, the dark will come, and you will find the strength you need."*

I opened my eyes to find Charles's gaze locked on mine, glossy as though my song had brought him to tears.

"That was beautiful," he whispered.

"Do you believe me now?"

He hesitated. "Yes."

My fingers twitched. I was tempted to reach for him. Not to hurt him, but to touch him, to feel his cool skin and the roughness of his stubble. Again, he rubbed his arm and shook it then rose to his feet. The symbols on my arm tingled, sending electrical surges through my body.

"What the-?" I ignored my hands—they were already healing anyway—and looked down to examine the symbols on my arm.

"What is it?" he asked, heading for the cage door with his key.

Before I could get a good look at the symbols, the squeal of crunching metal drew my attention to the back wall of the room. A door that I hadn't noticed before was suddenly ripped from its hinges and thrown behind an enraged Ashe and a very inconvenienced Zac.

In a blur, Ashe propelled straight into Charles, knocking him onto a workbench. They slid across it and off the other side with a thud, along with wrenches and rasps and screws that clanked, rattled, and tinkled as they hit the concrete floor.

I shot to my feet, almost grabbing the cage bars again and frustrated as hell when I remembered they were silver. "Stop, Ashe! Don't kill him! Zac, do something!"

He aimed his gun at the blurry mass of vampires rolling across the floor like two tomcats high on PCP.

"No! Don't shoot!" He wasn't listening. Ashe wasn't listening either. As soon as Zac had a clear shot, he'd take it. If Charles hesitated at all, Ashe would rip his head off.

Charles must have gotten the upper hand. One good side kick sent Ashe flying across the room. Zac took the shot, but Charles had already blurred back into Ashe. And they were at it again, throwing punches and kicks like an MMA fight gone berserk.

"Damn it!" Was this what it was like being a mother to a bunch of boys? It was enough to make me want to schedule a hysterectomy. I grabbed up the mattress, held it in front of me, and backed up as far as I could.

Then I charged. The hinges on the cage snapped, as did the lock. The door sailed through the air and slammed into a table saw. It must have hit the switch because the saw roared to life.

I flung the mattress aside and zipped past Zac, who was aiming his gun once again. Nope. I ripped the weapon from his hands, tossed it out of reach, and went for the brawling vampires. Somehow, I managed to get between them and struck out with both fists (and a nice scary battle cry, I might add). Ashe flew one way and Charles went the other. Both hit the floor and slid a few feet through the sawdust.

I'd moved so fast, Zac was still staring at his hand, his eyes wide until he looked up at me and did a double take. "Wren, are you okay?"

"Yeah, no thanks to you." I turned and pointed at Ashe and Charles in turn. "Or you. Or you."

Ashe shot to his feet and was at my side in the blink of an eye. I kept him at arm's length with a hand on his chest. Charles got up slowly, his eyes darting from Ashe to Zac. He backed up and stood a respectable, and safer, distance from us.

"Just tell me you're okay," Ashe said, his voice shaking and eyes still red with slow-dying rage.

"I'm okay. Charles isn't a threat."

"What do you mean he's not a threat?" Zac bellowed. Having found his gun, he racked the slide and held it down toward the floor with both hands, ready to fire if Charles so much as moved an inch in my direction.

"I can explain," he said quietly. "See, I was supposed to—"

Motorcycle engines growled outside on the gravel drive, getting louder the closer they came.

Charles zipped to the dirty window of the garage door and peeked out, ignoring Zac, who instantly aimed the gun at him. "You have to go. Take Wren and hurry!"

"Who is it, and why can't I have the pleasure of ripping their throats out?" I asked.

"Because you're not strong enough yet." He turned toward us, anger reddening his eyes. "I said, take her and go! Out the back, just get her the fuck out of here. I'll handle this. Go!"

"No! We can fight them!" I tried to go to him, but Ashe threw his arms around me.

He and Zac pushed me toward the back door, while Charles locked eyes with me one last time before they forced me outside and into the back seat of Birdie, where Ashe pinned me down.

Charles's horrendous scream sliced through my eardrums and stabbed my heart before the car door closed and drowned it out.

CHAPTER SIXTEEN

ASHE

RAGE, THE SEARING KIND that coiled across my shoulders and set my fangs on edge, continued to chew a hole through me miles after we left Charles and his woodshop. Part of me wanted to go back and tear Charles's throat out, slowly, until his head rolled free. Even though Wren sat next to me in the back seat of her car, completely unscathed—physically at least—he'd hurt her. Terrified her. I could still see the relief shining bright in her eyes at being away from him, could feel it in her death grip on my hand. Though she sat straight and stiffly alert, I could feel her body trembling through her leather jacket.

But while part of me wanted to go back and make sure he was dead, another part was just plain confused. Story of my life lately. Why had he had a sudden change of heart and let her go as soon as he heard motorcycle engines? I could still hear his screams echoing in my ears, the sound of his pain a strange mix of therapeutic and gut-churning.

A shudder raced down Wren's body, her side pressed tightly to mine. She must've been hearing the same echo.

I squeezed her hand tighter and traced little circles into the backs of her knuckles in an attempt to soothe her. And me.

"Are you all right?" I must've asked that same question about fifty times.

She nodded and offered a brief smile. Yeah, not sure I was buying it, but I'd do my best to give her the space she needed until she *was* all right.

"I'm fine. But what about him?" she asked.

"What *about* him? If he's not dead, he'll wish he was if I see him again."

"But I..." She rubbed her arm through the jacket. "Never mind."

I couldn't begin to know why she'd show that loser any mercy. Her heart was certainly more forgiving than mine. Maybe whatever he'd injected her with had affected her judgement.

"We've had a hell of the last few days," I said. "You'd think we'd be dead by now."

Wren's lips firmed as she stared hard out the window at the layers of fog. "Not even close."

Zac flicked his gaze to the rearview mirror. "It'll be sunrise soon. There's a motel about five miles up the highway."

"Or you could stop driving like an old man and get us to Brightwell," I said, scanning the horizon. A strip of dark blue had begun to creep into the night, as slow as the thick fog blanketing the road, but we still had time, and that was me being conservative. Still, I couldn't blame the guy for being overly cautious.

"It's your funeral," he shot back. "I'm driving the speed limit for a reason, you know."

"I know." I sighed into the breeze flowing in through the open window and pushed my fingers through my hair. "But it won't be anyone's funeral today, thanks to you."

He looked almost just as stunned as I felt at my good-enough thank you. He'd saved the day several times, but I still didn't like how he looked at Wren when he thought no one was looking. It reminded me way too much of how I probably looked at Wren.

"Wren?" he said. "You think we should go on to Brightwell?"

She turned to me, miscalculating how close my face was to hers, and brushing her lips against my chin in the process. Her mouth parted as her gaze dipped down, and when her eyes traced back up again, the symbol at my wrist heated and pulsed.

"You got a place to stay in Brightwell without any Ednas in a kitchen who'll rat us out?" she asked, and then licked her lips.

I followed the movement, and from the stirring in my jeans, so did my dick. "As a matter of fact, I do, and it's not too far from where I need to meet my sister."

"Okay," she said, and my symbol flamed hotter.

Zac pressed on the gas and sped us toward where the cops and Queen Ravana's minions would likely still be swarming the city to find me. But Jessica was there, too, and hopefully a few more answers that just might clear my name.

A vampire could sure hope.

The rumble of the car and the constant pulse at my wrist lulled me into a state of almost painful arousal. It was like our symbols were working to distract us from what had happened. Vampire Jesus, was it working. Wren squirmed in her seat next to me while her hand massaged the inside of my thigh. I could smell her sweet arousal as it filled the cab of the car, making me harder, making me want to grind against her. I wanted a bed so I could spread her wide, though, and a lot less of an audience, too.

When we made it there—with plenty of time to spare before sunrise, thank you very much—I guided Zac toward the rich neighborhood in Brightwell built around a small lake only about two miles from where I lived. Each three-story house had a private deck and beach in the back, and pruned hedges and fingerprint-free windows in the front.

Wren let out a low whistle as she made out the passing houses through the fog. "You live here?"

"No," I said, leaning forward in my seat to find what I was looking for.

"Oh." A crease formed on her forehead when she glanced over her shoulder at me. "So...we're here to measure our jealousy levels? Because I gotta say, color me unimpressed. I prefer small and cozy to this size." She squeezed my hand and winked. "In terms of houses, that is."

I snorted a laugh, but it quickly faded. We weren't here so I could impress her. Far from it. I hated large, gaudy houses, too, but it impressed me that Wren, a real queen, felt the same way. It didn't surprise me, seeing as how she'd grown up hiding in secret rooms in library basements and the like; it just... I don't know. Made her even more deserving of the title, more than I already thought she was? Made her more real and humble and therefore worthier than Queen Ravana who was rumored to literally run her many servants into early graves?

Wren would never do that. She was tough and lethal when she needed to be, but when she wasn't fighting for her life or someone else's, she was just Wren. Wren with an almost shy smile like the one she wore now, and soft curves pressed up next to me...

When a familiar house came into view over her head, I somehow tore my gaze from hers. "Zac. There. Turn your headlights off."

He did, and the fog closed in around us. Then he stopped and had to back up because we'd passed right by the house due to my Wren-trance. That was a tricky thing to snap out of.

With my vampiric sight, I guided Zac down a paved drive that ran parallel to the side of the house. I wasn't sure how shitty human eyesight was at night in the fog, but he trusted my lead enough to not question me. When he stopped, I hopped out to search for the key that would unlock the back gate. It wasn't hard since I'd been the one to put it inside the fake sprinkler head. After I unlocked the gate and climbed back into the car, both Zac and Wren were looking at me like I had a bit of flesh hanging from a fang.

"What?" I said.

"You're going to have to tell us how you know this place so well," Wren said. "Does a vampire version of Mrs. Robinson live here? Do you have a sugar momma?"

A sound almost like a laugh came from Zac as he pulled forward through the open gate, but that couldn't be right. The guy had one emotion—contempt. I must've been hearing things.

I clasped Wren's hand and scooted her closer to me. "No sugar mommas, just friendly vampires. I worked for this family in high school doing yard work and some cleaning while they traveled. Unfortunately—or fortunately, depending on how you look at it—their last name isn't Robinson. It's Anderson."

She nodded. "That's good."

"Jealous?"

"Damn right."

"You have no reason to be." And she really didn't. I was the one who should feel jealous of the four other guys who would complete her royal harem, who would touch her, taste her, and I *was* jealous. So to hear that she was, too, of an imaginary sugar momma shocked me, just one of a series of surprising jolts I'd had since I met her. It was weird and I couldn't explain it right, but it made me feel...important. Like I was so much more than an escaped prisoner accused of two murders I didn't commit.

Like I mattered to a true queen. Her first, and for now only, mate.

That was some pretty heavy shit, enough to pull me into yet another Wren-trance. She drew me in further with her smile, the way her lips moved when she said something to Zac.

"*Ashe*," Zac grinded out, as if this wasn't the first time he'd said my name.

I blinked away and found we were now parked on a drive in the sprawling backyard. "Yeah, just park it here. There are car covers in the guest house."

"Guest house?" Wren grinned. "Looks just like the regular house to me. Let me guess, this family uses summer as a verb, right?" She lifted her arm and flicked her wrist as if expecting a tuxedoed gentleman to kiss it. "Dahling, would you rather summer in the Hamptons or Hawaii?"

"Well...yeah." She'd pretty much nailed the Andersons' lifestyle and way of speaking, but the family had paid me really, really well. Even gave me access to the guest house and its fully stocked kitchen whenever I needed it, though I was pretty sure they'd meant when I was actually employed by them, not years after I'd left. A technical detail I chose to ignore, especially since they weren't here. They would be in Hawaii this time of year.

The guest house was tucked back against the far fence with ivy climbing up the eaves and tall, heavily draped windows with night blooming rose bushes in front of them. The key was hidden inside a tiny bird house hanging from a ceiling hook on the porch. I let us in, the cleaning chemicals inside burning my nose even though I wasn't inhaling. Whoever worked for the Andersons now didn't know the meaning of dilution, apparently.

I hit the light switch on the wall, which threw a soft glow on the modern chrome, granite, and wood, then double-checked I'd locked the door behind us. "The car covers are in the utility closet." I pointed down a hall to the left. "There are five bedrooms throughout the house, so take your pick. There might be human food in the fridge, Zac, but I can't guarantee it."

"Figures." He shook his head and started down the hall in the direction of the closet, his heavy footsteps thumping on the wood floor.

"I don't want my own bedroom, in case you didn't know." Wren stepped in close, one eyebrow lifted, and slid her lips along mine. Just a touch, but more than enough to stir everything right the fuck awake. Not difficult at all since my need for her started simmering just below my skin while we'd been in the back of the car, very literally at my wrist. Now, the symbol there pulsed in time with my throbbing cock.

I took her neck in my palm, my fingers gripping the hair at the back of her head, and dragged her closer to keep her there, connected to my body. Always. Her mouth moved with mine, just as soft and pliable as her body pressed up against me. She wrapped her arms around my neck with a desperate moan that nearly made me come from just the sound of it. I grabbed her ass and pulled her tight against me, the heat between her thighs spreading through my jeans and making me lose my mind. I moved my free hand under her shirt, under her bra, needing to feel every part of her tighten and squirm and shudder.

"I never did thank you properly for coming to rescue me." She pressed in closer, moving the both of us toward a dark doorway in the opposite direction Zac had gone. As her tongue slid against mine again, she moved her hand down over my jeans and squeezed my iron-hard dick.

"Wren..." It sounded like a warning, but it was more of a promise to her, like I was bowing in front of my queen with my fangs bared.

But then she was the one who was bowing, sinking down on her knees in front of me inside the dark room. The master bedroom, I realized, but then all my thoughts scattered at the sound of my zipper. When she took me into her mouth, pretty sure I almost left my body. Good thing I didn't though. Great thing, actually. Her lips and tongue glided up my dick, almost to the base, and then down to the tip again. And when she sucked in her cheeks and moaned, the vibration humming along every sensitive nerve... Sweet. Vampire. Jesus.

My hips thrust into her, slowly, as I cupped her head. I didn't want to hurt her, but I couldn't keep still either. I wanted to fuck her mouth hard. I wanted to bury myself inside her every which way. She didn't seem to mind though. In fact, she smiled up at me as much as she could with my cock in her mouth. A low groan barreled out of me as I thrust again, and again, each thrust met with Wren's wet tongue and lips sucking and licking. I held to her gorgeous face harder as I sped my pace, unable to control myself until an intensity unraveled deep inside me. I threw back my head and came into her mouth, my whole body buzzing like a thousand livewires.

I touched my fingers to her face. "My god, Wren."

"You're welcome. But also thank you. Again."

"Fucking any time."

She laughed, such a gorgeous sound.

It seemed to take hours to come back to my senses. I didn't know anything anymore, especially how, hours later, I woke up face-down on a bed with Wren tucked into my side. I supposed I'd passed out. Typical. And selfish. I'd make it up to Wren once she was awake.

In the meantime, I could suck the wings off a mosquito's thieving body, I was so hungry. My stomach was about to start a revolution. A glance at the wall clock showed me why. I'd slept for almost twelve hours.

I made my way to the kitchen where I found labeled, plastic-sealed packs of blood arranged by type in the refrigerator. I chose type A positive, which was the heartier, most savory of the types, in my expert, not-so-humble opinion.

There was also a sausage roll in there and an open box of Ritz crackers on the counter, so it looked like Zac had already dug in. I'd been kidding about the lack of human food in a vampire guest house. We would never starve our DBDs, not that he was. We weren't monsters. Most of us.

I heated a mug of blood in the microwave and then drank deep while I wandered into the darkened living room. Grayish evening daylight shined through the cracks in the heavy drapes, which at one time would've put me at ease that all was well and right with the world. But Queen Ravana's vampires had come to Edna's Itchen with the sun blazing down outside, which should've been impossible, but obviously it wasn't.

We weren't safe at any time of day, and most especially back in Brightwell. They would find us again. I had no doubts about that, but I hoped by then I would have some kind of proof that would clear my name. Or at least shine a different sort of spotlight on myself, one that revealed I'd only been trying to protect my sister, to fulfill a promise I'd made to her, and to keep her from making a mistake it turned out she wasn't even making. Not the greatest light, sure, but I hadn't even gone through with murdering Devin. Would I if he hadn't already been dead? Yes. Same with Charles, even though his screams haunted my dreams while I slept.

A light switched on behind me.

"Sleep well?"

I just about slopped the rest of the mug of blood all down my front. Zac, the bastard, had been sitting alone in the dark like a creeper.

"What the fuck, man?" I hissed. "Why are you just sitting there like that?"

He glared hard at me like he expected me to scream in terror or prepare myself for a long-winded lecture. Maybe both at the same time. "Why didn't you sense me with your preternatural abilities while I took first watch?"

Fair point, damn it. I'd been so focused with what might be lurking in the fog I didn't even spare a thought to what might already be inside the house.

"I got the watch from here." I dragged a black leather armchair to the window and sat with my back turned to him so he'd hopefully take the hint and leave.

No such luck.

"Do me a favor and try not to piss off the future queen so she doesn't stomp off again and get kidnapped. She was under your watch, Ashe. Keyword *watch*."

"Yeah. I get it. It won't happen again." He was right, damn him. I shouldn't have let her out of my sight in the library.

"You go where she goes," he snapped. "And now, I go where the both of you go until we're not constantly running for our lives."

I sighed and shook my head. "And if we never stop?"

"Then the three of us will be stuck like glue to each other, including tonight when you see your sister. Think you can handle that?"

Three was most definitely a crowd with this guy, but if it meant putting Wren in power in place of Queen Ravana, then yes. "If this whole glue thing also involves you gluing your mouth shut, then I can probably be talked into it. Not by you, obviously, but you get the idea."

"Uh-huh." He grunted as he rose from his chair. "You're a real funny one."

"What is your stake in all of this anyway?" I asked with a glance behind me. "Why do you care who's queen and who's not?"

"My stake is the same as yours. Sharp, pointy, and could go right through the heart if we're not careful."

"You're not a vampire. Try again."

"Like I said..." His footsteps sounded behind me as he crossed toward one of the bedrooms. "My stake is the same as yours."

"Are you always this cryptic when you're tired?" I shook my head. Dude must've been out of his mind with exhaustion, which made me feel only slightly guilty that I'd crashed first. But really, what *was* his deal, anyway? He was like a dam of muscles holding back a river of secrets. As long as those secrets kept Wren alive until she took the throne, then I'd give him his space, I guess.

Just before eleven thirty at night, Wren woke Zac while I kept watch, and then the three of us slipped out into the night to go meet my sister. Like the night before, fog clung to the air, only thicker. It was a good cover for us, though, while we walked to my old house, moving like silent shadows. We kept to the cover of trees and bushes mostly and avoided the commercial streets altogether. The fog smothered any noise we made, but it would also quiet the sounds of anyone coming after us.

I kept my eyes and ears sharp. None of us spoke hardly a word, and when we did, it was at a whisper.

When we hopped the fence into the backyard of my old house, my cell phone buzzed in my pocket, about 4000 decibels quieter than it had in the library. I fished it out, fully expecting it to be Jessica cancelling her Hogwarts visit with me tonight.

But no. It wasn't. It was Marta, possibly with news of the security footage in our apartment building. If my heart ever beat, it would have crashed through my ribs right now.

I pressed Wren and me to a wide tree trunk next to the turreted garden shed before I took the call, grabbing her hand for luck. Zac disappeared into the fog, but I could still feel his contempt spiking through my chest.

"Marta," I whispered, "light of my life, tell me you have good news."

Wren's brows climbed up her forehead as she stared at me, her expression fiery.

I squeezed her hand harder, willing her to trust me.

"Well, Ashley," Marta started. "I have good news and I have great news. Which would you like first?"

Good thing I had the bulk of the tree at my back because my legs about gave out with a surge of relief. "Both. All at once."

Marta clicked her tongue, and I could feel her smile through the phone. "I'll do my best. There's grainy footage of two men in the hallway outside your apartment door. Grainy because they spray-painted over the cameras but were sloppy about it. Neither of them were you. One is holding what looks to me like a silver net in gloved hands. That's the good news."

I sank my eyes closed and grinned. "And the great news?"

"An outside camera at Dora's Flowers across the street shows two shadows inside your apartment seconds after the first video was taken."

My grin spread to an eardrum-cracking one, and I opened my eyes to stare at Wren. "I could kiss you right now."

Wren had lost her pissed-off fire, seeming to read between the lines of the one-way conversation she'd just heard, and a deep crease formed on her forehead as she studied me.

"Yeah, well, you better make time for the kissing, mister, but only after you clear your name," Marta warned.

"Yes. About that. Is there a way you can send the videos to me?"

"No, I can't. But I figured you'd ask that, and my son, Dominic, is working on that right now. Remember Dominic?"

"I remember." Dumb as a rock and just as lazy. My phone chimed in my ear. "I think I just got them. That was fast. You're a literal lifesaver, Marta."

"Uh-huh. I know. Which means you're coming to Thursday's bridge club? For my kiss while I'm kicking your ass?"

"If I can make it, I'll be there. Thank you. I mean it."

"Go save the day, Ashley." She hung up, and my fingers shook as I opened her son's texts. Instead of looking at them myself, I thrust the phone to Wren.

"My apartment," I said.

Her fingers folded around mine as she took it, her eyes filled with questions as she gazed down. After a moment, she shook her head and smiled. "It doesn't change anything for me. I knew deep down you were innocent when you told me you didn't murder my mother." She handed the phone back. "But it does change everything for you."

"It does. I mean, it *could* if Queen Ravana doesn't get her hands on it and 'accidentally' destroys it or something."

"Ashe." The voice came out of the fog, disembodied but familiar.

I turned and caught my sister's form emerge like some kind of specter from another dimension. She'd come. I supposed I didn't have any reason to doubt she would, but seeing her now standing next to Hogwarts, right after I'd been at my lowest and most scared, brought me back to a simpler time when I wasn't running for my life.

It also cracked open my voice a little when I said, "Jessica..."

Wren's hand fluttered to my back as she moved deeper into the fog to give us privacy, her brief touch soothing.

Jessica wore a flannel shirt and jeans, her long blonde hair up high in her usual ponytail. "I heard voices."

"It's just me." Explaining Wren and Zac was too much right now, and they'd hidden themselves anyway.

She stepped closer as tears sprang to her eyes. "Why are you so stupid sometimes, Ashe?"

I barked out a strange laugh and shook my head. "Because I'm your little brother. I didn't kill Devin. I was given bad information, a photo of you and him taken years ago instead of weeks, with the wrong date on it to trick me."

"Then you should've come to me instead of turning vigilante to protect a sister you don't trust enough to take care of herself." Her tone was sharp yet strangled as her chin wobbled. "I'm not stupid. I've made exactly two mistakes in my entire life, and one of them *wasn't* going back to Devin."

She was right, of course. I hadn't trusted her not to go back to him, which is why I'd hired Charles to keep an eye on her in the first place. Our communication had never been great, though, and I doubted she would have ever told me Devin was abusive before I saw the evidence myself.

"Seeing what he did to you that day..." I swallowed hard.

She blinked up at the turrets of Hogwarts and placed her palm against its wall. "I know what it did to you. I saw it happening to you. My pain became your pain, and...I'm sorry for that."

"You have no reason to be sorry."

She shook her head, her tears flowing freely now as she looked at me once again. "You want to know what my second mistake was?"

I shrugged. "Sure."

"I should've been your friend, Ashe, not just a shitty big sister."

"You weren't shitty. You were..." How to phrase this so she wouldn't hate me?

She laughed, the sound wet and hollow and a little devastated. "Shitty, but I promise to try to do better."

"Me too." And I meant it. I could've made an effort to be her friend too. Maybe, if I had, she would've confided in me *before* things turned so explosive with Devin. It shouldn't have been her bruised face that brought out the brother in me. I should've been there for her all along, and knowing that I hadn't been would weigh heavily on my shoulders for a literal eternity. "I swear."

"What happens now?" she asked, wiping her face. "Are you leaving?"

"I'm not sure, actually. Queen Ravana seems to really want me out of the way, and yet, here I am. I have evidence that clears me from Queen Bronwen's murder, but I was still at the scene of the crime at Devin's."

"Funny, I thought I saw Queen Bronwen standing right next to you when I got here. You sure she's not haunting you out of revenge?"

I laughed but didn't confirm or deny that. I figured the less Jessica knew about Wren and her rightful crown, the better and safer she'd be.

"What kind of evidence?" she asked.

"Video of two guys in my apartment."

A loud police siren filled the night, sharp and quick like a bullet. Like a warning. Like a breaking dam funneling in all my nightmares.

"Time to go," Zac hissed from somewhere in the fog.

"Who is that?" Jessica whispered.

Sounds echoed through the dark, like heavy footsteps but the fog misplaced them, made it hard to tell how close and how many.

I snapped my attention back to Jessica. Her eyes were wide, shocked, still wet with tears. She hadn't called them here. I felt that bone-deep, just as much as I felt whoever was coming would find and destroy the evidence on my phone.

"Take this." I crossed to her and crushed my phone into her hand. "The videos are on it. Blast them to the press. Quick as you can."

"But what about y—"

"Jessica." I took her by the elbows, relieved at how sturdy she felt. Not breakable at all. Not anymore. "Don't worry about me. I'm not done annoying my big sister."

"Okay. I-I love you." She gripped the phone tight as she threw her arms around me.

Squeezing her hard to me, I whispered, "I love you too. Now, run." Then I let her go to face the rest of the night.

CHAPTER SEVENTEEN

WREN

TWO THINGS WERE CERTAIN. One: we were on the run again. Old news by now. And two: There was indeed a second symbol on my arm, another blue diamond shape just like the one that appeared when I found Ashe. The light and pulsing from it weren't nearly as strong as that of Ashe's symbol, but I was ninety-eight-point five percent certain I knew whose it was. Did it mean that he was still alive? It had to. I felt it beyond the symbol. Like when we'd gotten within a few miles of Ashe. But it was faint. So much so, I couldn't tell which way to go.

Ashe fell asleep as we rode in the back seat of Birdie while Zac once again drove us to parts unknown. Ashe's head rested against my shoulder, but tension still pulled at his eyes and mouth. Poor guy was exhausted, but worried sick about his sister and probably me too.

I wasn't used to worrying about anyone but myself, but my worry list was growing by the minute. How could

I know for certain whether Charles was still alive? Was Ashe's sister now in jail, dead, or worse yet, being tortured so they could get to him? What was Zac's stake in all of this beyond daytime reconnaissance, bodyguard, and getaway driver? He had to have bills to pay or something. But who was paying him? Not me. For a queen, I had some mighty empty pockets. The little cash I had was dwindling fast from gas money alone. I'd have to get another gig soon and figure out what Zac had to gain from being part of a vampire drama.

The thing that worried me most at that moment, however, was how to tell Ashe that I may have found my second mate. My brain must have short-circuited trying to make sense of everything. The car's dark interior faded away into a haze of bitter cold and the smell of death.

And I was back in the crypt on that awful night just after sunset. My stomach growled painfully. In two days of hiding, our only food had been one still-twitching, snow-dusted raccoon that had been hit on the road beside the cemetery the night before. It was so cold that its blood had turned to slush and barely quelled our hunger enough to allow us to sleep through the next day.

But on this night, Mama and I were wrapped in the blue tarp, propped up against the wall. She was still asleep. I sat motionless, watching as a scrawny rat wandered in, nibbled at some crumbs on the floor, and crept toward me.

As soon as it was within reach, I snatched it up, broke its neck, and bit into it, taking big, slow gulps of its hot blood. I had almost drained it when Mama stirred then opened her eyes.

"Want some, Mama?" I showed her the rat, thinking she'd be proud of me for my first kill.

"Did you get that all by yourself?" She sat up, smiling as she took the rat from me and brought her mouth to its neck. Then she paused, sniffing it. Her eyes widened just as pain speared my stomach. Everything came back up in violent retching. I thought my insides might come out too.

My mother panicked. She searched around the crypt, gasped, and squatted down next to the little pile of crumbs where the rat had just been. "Oh no. No, no, no!"

"What's wrong, Mama?" I said between gagging. Pain and terror pulled tears from my eyes and down my cheeks, where they froze like tiny icicles on my jaw.

"We have to find you some better food right now, okay?" She bit her wrist and offered me some of her blood. It eased my stomach enough to stave off the vomiting. Then she wrapped the tarp around me tightly. Scooping me up in her arms, she carried me to the barred door of the crypt and peeked out before easing it open. She winced as the rusty hinges squeaked into the freezing silence of the cemetery. Then, she continued through the door into the snow.

There must have been six inches on the ground. It made a *shush, shush, shush* sound as she trudged through it. The moonlight twinkled across the snow, making it sparkle like a blanket of diamonds. It was so beautiful. The snow-capped gravestones cast long shadows across the ground. Blue, wispy ghosts darted between the stones, peeking out to watch the starving vampires seek their last supper.

I waved and smiled at them. We hadn't been there long enough for me to make any friends, like I had with Chip, but I thought we'd have plenty of time to get to know one another. I was wrong.

My mother found a homeless man in an alley, half frozen and unconscious, but still alive, shivering beneath a few layers of cardboard and dirty blankets. I couldn't remember the last time we'd fed from a human. She pierced his jugular with her fangs and gently pushed me down to drink. I looked up at her as my lips made contact. It was already warm and delicious, but something didn't feel right. She was nervous, her gaze darting all around us.

She smiled down at me. "Drink, baby. Hurry. He can't feel it. He's already dying, so we're helping him be at peace."

Next thing I knew, I was torn from the frigid past and back in the car. Cool fingers were tracing across the skin on my arm. I screamed and bolted across the seat until my back hit the side panel, kicking at whomever had invaded the space. My boot made contact with something. It crunched. Someone cried out. The car swerved.

"What the fuck?!" Zac barked, finally getting the car under control enough to slow down and pull off the road.

When the car came to a stop, Ashe opened the door and stumbled out of the car, holding his jaw.

"Oh shit! Ashe!" I opened the door and ran around the back of the car.

Ashe held his other hand up to ward me off.

"What did you do to her?" Zac's growling accusation preceded him as he rounded the front of the car, gun drawn.

"Ask *her*," Ashe said, his words slurred. Blood dripped from between his fingers.

I got between them. "Put the gun down, Zac, for shit's sake. He didn't do anything to me. It was..." Fuck, I didn't even know what it was. A dream? A vision? A memory? "I'm sorry. Seriously."

"I'll be fine," Ashe said. "Just...give me a minute."

He didn't say it, but I knew that meant *stay the fuck away from me*. How was I supposed to be anyone's mate, much less a queen, if I spazzed out and broke whoever's jaw was closest to me?

Ashe wandered farther off the road into the woods and leaned up against a tree, rolling his neck from side to side. He was in pain, and it hurt me to the core that I'd caused it.

"Wren?" Zac's quiet voice behind me made me jump.

I spun around.

His hand hovered over his gun, one foot behind the other in a defensive stance. "Take it easy."

Great, he was scared of me too. I lowered my head and rested my butt on Birdie's trunk. "Maybe don't sneak up on me next time, especially if I've just spazzed out?"

"Noted. But what happened?"

Glancing over to where Ashe had wandered, I couldn't see him anymore, which was either a good or bad thing. I didn't want to go chasing after him, for fear of him thinking I was coming to finish him off. I pulled up my jacket sleeve, where the symbols glowed softly in the dark night, Ashe's brighter than the other.

Zac, eyeing me uneasily, slowly came closer and inspected them. "Number two? When did that happen?"

"When I was caged in the woodshop."

"Him?"

"I think so, yeah."

"Or, maybe..."

"What?"

He scratched the back of his neck, peering around us at the dark countryside where crickets, cicadas, and a distant dog conversed in the summer night. "Could have been one of the others."

"The guys on motorcycles?"

"Yeah."

"No, it can't be."

"Ravana could have persuaded a potential mate to her side. It's happened before."

"It has? When?"

"Did you see a symbol on *his* arm?"

"Yeah...I mean, no." A sudden thought struck. "But he *was* rubbing and shaking his arm as though there might be something there."

"Maybe you injured him?"

I walked away a few paces, doubt now trickling down my neck along with the humid air condensing on my cool skin. "He let me go. Why would he if he didn't realize he was my mate?"

"I don't know. What did you say to him before that?"

"I convinced him that I was Bronwen's daughter. He asked me questions only she and I would know. I answered them. How would he know to ask those if he wasn't connected to me?"

"Someone with enough motive to get to you could have given him the information. But that was enough to change his mind?"

"I guess so, but why, unless he's my mate?"

"I've done a little digging on Charles Ford. He's a notorious gambler, womanizer, and bounty hunter. The price on your head would have paid off all his gambling debts and then some. Maybe once he knew you were the real deal, there was a better buyer he had in mind."

"Better than Ravana? Who else would benefit from keeping me prisoner?"

He shrugged, but the way his eyes flicked to the side, I knew he wasn't telling me everything.

"So you think he'll try to kidnap me again?"

An owl hooted from a tree above us. It reminded me that we were never truly alone. Zac must have realized that too.

"We need to go."

"But where? Listen, Detective, I'm tired of being escorted to one unknown location to another without having a clue where we're going or why."

"Understood. We'll talk in the car."

"No, we'll talk now. What do you have to gain from helping me with this?"

"It's my job. All I can tell you now is that the FBI and SFBI are working together to find all the human-vampire connections leading to a rise in corruption and mysterious disappearances."

"The SFBI?"

"Like I said, we'll talk about it later. Ashe, time to go!" Zac called toward the woods where Ashe had escaped the wrath of my boot to his face.

Nothing moved. I felt the panic rising like sour bile into my throat. Had he run away? Been captured? I started for the woods, leaping over the ditch as bushes rustled, and Ashe emerged. I hesitated a moment, then ran to him, stopping at arm's length. He stood still, his jaw seemingly fine. Blood stained his shirt and lingered on his neck. His eyes were full of questions, doubts, fears. And I'd put them there.

"I'm so sorry," I whispered. "I never meant to hurt you."

He swallowed hard. "I know."

I closed the gap and wrapped my arms around his neck. He held me tight, his fingers pressing into me as though fighting the urge to push me away.

"Are you okay?" I pulled away just enough to look at his face. Still just as gorgeous as ever.

"I am now. It's healing."

He smiled, revealing a small gap where his left fang should have been. "Oh no. Will it grow back?"

"Maybe. I'm due for another dentist appointment anyway."

Zac cleared his throat. We all piled into Birdie and drove wordlessly for a little while. Ashe sat close to me, holding my hand, fingers intertwined with mine. At least he didn't hate me. Yet.

"We're headed to Faymont, Mississippi," Zac said, breaking the silence.

"Why?" Ashe asked.

"There's an underground nightclub. It's known for illegal gambling and all the usual debauchery, plus whatever vampires do in there."

Ashe groaned. "The Stake and Dagger."

"Yes, that's the one."

Ashe pinched the bridge of his nose. "Shit. We can't take Wren in there. It's dangerous for even us nobodies. She'll be recognized immediately."

I watched Zac's smile stretch across his face in the mirror.

"No, she won't," he said. "Neither will we. Melody Songsmith needs a new gig. We'll come along and be her roadies."

"Wait, what?"

I realized I hadn't really told Ashe about my alter ego. We still had so much to learn about each other.

"Don't worry," I said. "You'll look good with black hair, I think."

We spent the next hundred miles talking about my singing job. Ashe, I discovered, had played the drums for a while in a garage band. Zac could actually play the harmonica. He could even carry a decent tune, as he showed us singing along to Queen's "Bohemian Rhapsody" on the radio.

"How are we going to get a gig there?" I asked.

"Don't worry, I'll take care of that," Zac said. "Just rest. You'll need a good meal and a good day's sleep before we step foot in there."

We drove on, the only noise coming from a staticky country station on the radio. Unexpected tears burned my eyes as the weight of what had happened over the past few hours kicked in. But I didn't let them fall. Even when I realized the dream that had prompted me to break my mate's jaw wasn't a dream at all.

Ashe leaned in and whispered, "We're going after your next mate, aren't we? I saw the new symbol on your arm.

I was touching it when you woke up and kicked me. Were you having a nightmare?"

I nodded and turned toward the window, watching the dark fields whipping by, the distant yellow lights of homes full of warm bodies. Moms, dads, kids, dogs — families who had normal troubles like car payments and not making the cheerleading squad.

"Actually, no. It was more than just a nightmare. It was a memory of that night. The night my mother died."

"What did you remember?"

I bit my lip, but the truth was too bitter to keep inside anymore. "It's my fault that she's dead."

CHAPTER EIGHTEEN

ASHE

"IT'S NOT YOUR FAULT." I tried to reach for her, but she swatted my hand away, her eyes shining with tears. "Wren, you didn't kill your mother."

"No, but it's my fault she was killed." Her voice rose, pleading for me to understand, and I was trying to.

I'd never seen her so broken, though. Lethal and terrifying while facing the last few days, soft and pliant while pressed up against me, but never broken.

When she'd composed herself, she continued. "I was trying to prove to her that she'd trained me well, that she could be proud of me, and I caught a rat. I was so excited to show it to her. She'd always taught me to feed myself first. 'Take care of you,' she'd say, and I did. But then I got sick. Mom woke up, saw the rat, and she knew..."

I took her hand, already seeing where this was going. My stomach tightened and curled like I was there with her in the past.

"Rat poison," Zac muttered from the driver's seat.

Wren nodded. "She said I needed better food to counter the poison, so we slinked out into the night, out from hiding, I later realized, and found a homeless man in an alley. Even though I felt better after that, something in the air didn't feel right. Mom felt it too. Her eyes kept darting everywhere. She told me to run and hide, to play silent as the grave, she said. We'd practiced it so many times. I hid in a dumpster at the end of the alley, didn't move a muscle, didn't bat an eye. And then...they came."

I sank my eyes closed because now I understood where the blame for herself came from. Still unfounded, but understandable since she'd been so young at the time.

"Her attackers came right out from a side door in one of the buildings as if they'd been waiting there the whole time. A whole group of them with a silver net and silver spears. They staked her everywhere but her heart fifty-seven times right in front of me, hidden from view, but I could still see everything." She looked straight ahead and swallowed, as if seeing it all again.

I slid my hand across the seat and touched her fingertips. "She made a choice to save you, her daughter, knowing that you were worth the risk."

She shook her head, her tears flowing faster. "I was stupid."

"You were a kid who had no way of knowing what would happen next."

"She might still be alive today if I'd just made one choice differently."

"But you didn't." I undid my seat belt so I could wrap her up against me, and our bodies fit perfectly while she clung to me. "Neither did she, and I bet she'd make the same choice if she had to do it again."

She went quiet for a long time, the deep groove between her eyebrows never relaxing, but her tears dried. I hated to see her hurt like this, had felt like each one of her tears was like a blade cutting open my heart. So, as long as she needed to be held, I would be right here.

THE THREE OF US left a literal hole-in-the wall hotel looking nothing like we had when we arrived. Zac and I wore short, itchy wigs, colored contacts, a fang implant from my unfortunate meeting with Wren's foot, and—get this—makeup. Never in my life had I let a woman "contour" my face, "shade in" my eyebrows, or tell me that my eyelashes made her want to apply mascara to me.

No way on the mascara. A guy had to draw the line somewhere. I had to admit, though, when I looked in the mirror, my whole face appeared to have changed shape. It was a little unnerving staring at the face of a stranger, but if I fooled myself, I figured I would fool most people.

And Wren... She was gorgeous before, but now with her eyes painted so they had these dramatic wings and her short black wig, she reminded me of a panther, all sleek and grace and hot as fuck.

While we rode in the back of a taxi to The Stake and Dagger, my hand on her knee, and a raging boner begging to be freed, it took every bit of restraint not to part her thighs and start humping like a rabid animal. I knew she could sense everything going through my head because the instant I saw her as Melody Songsmith, the symbol on my wrist had flared. Hers had, too, because she stopped like she'd hit a wall and stared down at it, and then up at me with a sinful grin curling her mouth.

"Down, boy," she'd said.

Yeah, not any time soon.

The taxi pulled up in front of the club, which was out in the middle of a country highway, and I wished we were anywhere else. This club, an innocent-looking one-story slab of stone, was actually a secret underground vampire bar underneath a human bar accessible by only an underground tornado shelter. The only reason I knew about it was because of my friend Jake from high school who'd overheard his uncle talking about it. We drove here once with the intent to test out our new fake IDs, but when the guy waiting in front of us didn't know the password to get through the basement door, the bouncer killed him.

Jake and I, properly freaked, went back to my place and played a role-playing game called Felons and Fangs like good little boys.

Now, the human part of the club beat a steady bass I could feel through the taxi's tires, a beacon to the gullible. Like us. We were fucking doomed. Sure, we needed money to continue running, but there were plenty of other clubs Wren could perform at. None of them were this one, which meant I was already a huge fan of all clubs not named The Stake and Dagger.

Yet, here we were.

There were only a few cars parked out front, the night too young yet for all but the hard-core clubbers. No one seemed to be dying or on the verge of death, so that was good.

When we retrieved Wren's guitar from the taxi trunk and it drove off without us, I turned to Wren. "Does anyone even know the password?"

"Isn't the password always password?" Zac asked, and I couldn't tell if he was fucking joking.

Wren put a hand on my chest. "Relax."

"I doubt that's happening." But like I always did, I tried to blend in with my surroundings, make it not only look like I belonged but was damn happy to be here. It was a struggle, let me tell you.

We walked up to the tornado shelter door, and a big bald guy sitting nearby in the bed of his truck. Zac crossed over and flashed him what looked like a business card, and the guy waved us on without a word.

All that worrying for nothing.

We strode down the shelter steps and inside the bar, the music thumping louder from both above ground and below.

A guard with a harelip scar who was dressed in a blood-red three-piece suit stepped in front of us and held his hand up. "Leave your weapons at the door."

Shit. *There* was a reason to worry.

"What weapons?" Zac asked, playing dumb.

The guard gave him a "cut the bullshit" look.

Another guard walked around behind him. "Hands up, wide stance."

Zac rolled his eyes as the guy patted him down and (of course) found his holstered gun. He took the gun and handed it over to his partner, then patted Zac down some more. It wouldn't take much for the guards to discover that we were in disguise, but a few impatient women who clomped down the steps behind us made him speed up the search.

He patted me down, finding nothing, because I had no weapons apart from my good looks.

Then it was Wren's turn. When he got a little too close to her breast, she growled, "Hey, watch it if you want to keep that hand."

The guard finished quickly and waved us inside. If all went as planned, we wouldn't need a gun anyway.

Only a few high-top tables were occupied, and even fewer booths along the right wall. The bar stood to the left with two vampires behind it slinging drinks, and straight ahead through the curls of cigarette smoke sat an elevated stage. The colored overheads spotlighted the duct tape holding the microphone to the stand and the scuff marks through half an inch of dust on the stage floor.

I caught Wren's eye, and she shrugged.

"I've performed in worse," she said.

"I'll go find the manager. Let her know you're here." Zac stalked off toward the bar.

Wren and I sat at a nearby table. She propped her guitar case on a chair, her attention straying to the mildly curious faces turning toward us.

"Nervous?" I asked.

She craned her neck to look at those sitting at the bar behind her and then flicked her stunning gaze at me. "I don't get nervous before a show. I just..." She rubbed at the symbol on her wrist with her thumb.

"Yeah." I felt it too. A prickling sensation centered in a different spot on my symbol, not unlike the feeling that runs up the back of your neck when someone's watching. Which I hoped to Vampire Jesus they weren't.

Zac came back a second later. "Okay. It's showtime when you're ready, Wr—Melody. One song to see how these yahoos like you."

"Just one?" I asked. "Should you wait until these guys are good and hammered?"

"At least give me a *little* credit." Wren gave me a teasing smile as she stood.

"No, that's not what I—" I started, but she'd already headed toward the stage.

Well, shit. My intent had come out all wrong.

Zac slapped me in the chest while giving me a go-to-hell look. "You've never heard her sing, roadie. Now, come and help me do whatever it is roadies do."

Zac and I followed Wren up the few steps onto the stage. I carried her guitar so it looked like I was actually useful and set it down by a speaker. The music quieted, the loud voices softened some, and chairs scooted behind us in anticipation. Zac went straight for the taped-up microphone which had flopped down to the side like a sad dick, grabbed a nearby roll of duct tape and wrapped it around the microphone until it stood up like an excited dick. He ripped the tape strip with his teeth, grinning up at me as if to say I wasn't the only one with a dangerous bite.

"Wren, I'm sorry," I whispered as I swooped in on some extension cords that lay on the stage. They didn't seem to be attached to anything but each other.

She touched my shoulder and smiled, the colored lights reflecting the excitement in her eyes. "It's fine. Really. I knew what you meant."

I deposited the bundle of cords behind a speaker so she wouldn't trip over them. "Then break a leg."

"I will." She broke out in a grin, an infectious one, and I couldn't help but notice how at home she appeared up here, about to perform. "Have a seat and relax."

Some guy came up to the stage and asked her a question about the sound and some other technospeak. She hooked up her guitar to the amp, and then having no idea what else to do, Zac and I made our way to the bar to enjoy the show.

A burst of feedback squawked through the microphone. Wren winced, then leaned in and introduced the song. "Good evening. This is one of the lesser known songs by Janis Joplin, called 'Little Girl Blue.'" And then, without any introduction, Wren opened with a soulful guitar riff.

The chatter died down as the bar patrons started paying attention. Low and throaty, Wren's voice filled the bar with a song I'd never heard before. She sounded like smoke and silk and sex, like light and dark, all coming from inside a place I hadn't known existed in my favorite vampire queen.

Wow.

When she'd said she could sing, I didn't imagine it would sound like *this*.

I turned from my seat at the bar and looked around at everyone else's expressions. Most leaned forward and listened as hard as they could. Some wore dreamy smiles, and others tapped their feet in time with the

music. She had all of them under her power, including Zac sitting next to me, his gaze aimed at the steps
leading toward the stage and a relaxed version of his
kill-you-later expression on his face. That was a first, all
because of Wren.

When the last note faded, the bar erupted with applause and glass-banging on the tables and bar. She'd
definitely grabbed her one-song chance by the balls. I
didn't know it was possible to feel this proud of anyone
in my life.

With her excited grin still locked in place, she made
her way off the stage but got caught up by several of her
new fans.

Zac hopped off his bar stool. "I'll go make sure nobody
gets too friendly."

I nodded, about to join him, but an image on the
TV screen on the wall above the bartender caught my
attention.

A still shot of my sister on the local news channel.

Questions flooded my head so fast I went numb. I
sat, unmoving, every part of my body tensed while I
tried to grasp what I was seeing. Not once had I said
she had to *go to* the news station, just to send them the
videos proving my innocence. So what was she doing
in a cinderblock interrogation room that looked like the
one I'd been in after I was arrested?

"Can you turn on closed captioning?" I asked the
bartender, my voice surprisingly collected while worry
chewed its way through my gut. Whatever was happening, I didn't want the sound on so the whole bar could
hear.

The bartender did at the same time the still shot turned into a video.

"My brother didn't kill Queen Bronwen or Devin," my sister said, her words scrolling across the bottom. "If these videos I've shown you don't clear his name of Queen Bronwen's murder, then I have something else that will clear him of Devin's. Email exchanges, money transfers, all to an anonymous assassin hired to take out Devin. Hired by *me*." She glanced up at the camera in the corner of the room, her eyes so much like mine looking right at me, a sad smile on her face. She patted what looked like her closed laptop that sat balanced on her knees. "All right here."

I covered my mouth with my fist so I wouldn't make a sound. Jessica, my own sister...*had hired an assassin to kill her ex-boyfriend*. This was insane. Almost as insane as her younger brother wanting to do it first. That explained why Devin was already dead when I got there. Had this assassin nearly killed me, too, in their hurry to get out of there?

This was too much. All this time, I'd been obsessed with making sure Jessica didn't make the same mistake twice with Devin. I'd made the choice to save her the second I saw her beaten and broken. Just like she'd made the choice to come forward to the police and save me now. My own sister had stepped forward to take the blame off of me.

My chest seemed to cave in with frustration, with love, both the same side of the coin when it came to Jessica. My eyes stung, and I was glad I was alone to feel all of this.

Jessica and I had made a choice to save each other. Hadn't I just said something similar to Wren about her mom? Life—such as it was—seemed to be a series of choices all revolving around the people we loved. I'd already chosen to save the Southern Clan of the Vampire Nation by putting Wren in power. Yet another choice I'd made out of love.

All right here, Jessica had said, and maybe I was reading too much into it, but the way she'd said it, facing the camera with a smile, made me think it was a message. *All right here*. But she wouldn't be. Not if she was already in an interrogation room. The police would charge her with murder if they hadn't already.

The symbol on my wrist tingled, announcing Wren's presence before she touched my shoulder.

"Hey, you okay?" she said, her voice concerned.

I nodded and cleared my throat, blinking hard to regain some composure. "All right here."

Her grip on my shoulder tightened at the same time my wrist prickled again, sharp and unpleasant. Her wide eyes aimed past me.

I turned to look and was met with a wall of vampire topped with a dusty leather fedora.

Charles Fucking Ford. Liar. Lady killer. Wren's kidnapper. The bane of my existence.

He yanked up his brick-red shirt sleeve from around his wrist and slapped his arm down on the bar in front of us. A faintly glowing symbol inked his skin. A symbol *just like mine*.

"Looks like this gets me in your club?" he said.

My jaw fell into my lap as I faced Wren. "*Him?*"

"I sure as hell didn't choose him." She flicked her gaze to him and glared. "I'd hoped he was dead."

He grinned, a real shit-eating one too. "Sorry to disappoint, darlin'. All I know is, ever since you took off with her, she's done nothing but give me wet dreams."

I dared a look at Wren to gauge her reaction, and I wish I hadn't. Her eyes were glued to his, her tongue flicked across her lips as though she wanted to jump his bones right there on the bar.

No, this couldn't be right.

With someone like him in Wren's harem, someone with fewer morals than a rock and zero fucks given other than for dollar signs, we stood no chance putting Wren on the throne. With him, we were Fucked—capitalized, outlined in red, spotlighted, and placed on a pedestal.

"About the not being dead thing..." I rose and faced him, my fists clenched at my sides. "Maybe we could fix that. Right here. Right now."

ABOUT THE AUTHORS

MYSTI PARKER IS AN award-winning author and shameless chocoholic. She writes romance for every reader's taste from super sweet to scandalously spicy. When she's not writing the next best-story-ever or tackling the endless mountain of laundry, she works as a freelance copywriter and editor. Mysti resides in Louisville, Kentucky with her husband, three children and too many pets.

Website: www.mystiparker.com

LINDSEY R. LOUCKS IS an award-winning, *USA Today* bestselling author of paranormal romance, science fiction, and contemporary romance. When she's not discussing books with anyone who will listen, she's dreaming up her own stories. Eventually her brain gives out, and she'll play hide and seek with her cat, put herself in a chocolate-induced coma, or watch scary movies alone in the dark to re-energize.

Website: www.lindseyrloucks.com

Milton Keynes UK
Ingram Content Group UK Ltd.
UKHW010715080823
426520UK00001B/22